Insurrections

Sal Hunter

ISBN 9798759362814

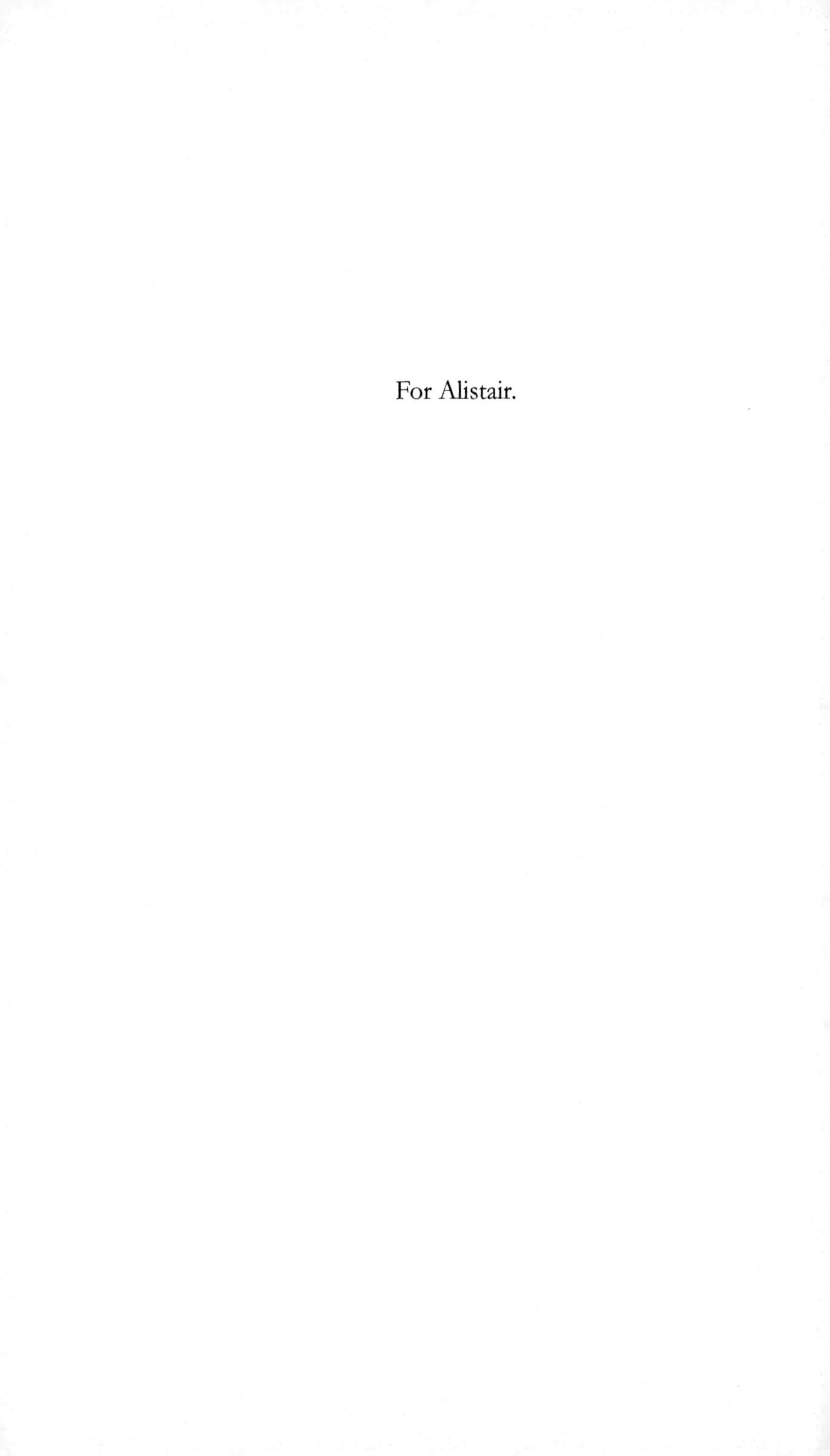

For Alistair.

Contents

Chapter 1 – Sunday 16th December

Blinking hard, relieved to be alone at last but knowing she needed to concentrate, Bev checked the busy junction one last time before carefully pulling out - straight into the path of an oncoming bus. She grasped what she had done seconds too late, slamming on her brakes and stopping her outsize car, but still the bus was too close and had to swerve dramatically to avoid her. Heaving breath into her lungs and mortified by her lack of attention, Bev shook her head and tried to ignore the adrenaline tingling across the backs of her hands. The bus driver didn't stop, familiarity for once breeding acceptance. As the cars behind her started to beep their horns, she checked again and pulled away safely, chastising herself to be more careful. It had been a tiring few days, and she couldn't afford to lose concentration now.

She breathed evenly and deeply, focused on the road, but still enjoying the blue skies overhead and unusually mild day. Her short-sleeved top would be hidden by knitwear for the next few months, but today her arms could be bare in the sunshine through the car windows. In the distance, she caught sight of the eclectic architecture of central Glasgow and grinned affectionately at its concrete and spires. There, locals would be enjoying their Sunday morning brunches and strolls, relishing the day in a way she couldn't. At least they were happy, she thought.

Shortly beforehand, she had dropped Lana and Munro at their car, leaving them to complete their homeward journey alone. Both were giddily relieved that Lana was no longer at threat of being picked up by the police and committed to hospital care. Bev let loose a huff of breathy laughter, realising that this was the first time that her career choice had enabled her to help someone she knew - she often thought tradespeople must have the highest number of friends. Even so, it had been hard for Bev to celebrate with the others the night before: for them, the evening marked the end of an ordeal, but for her it was a potential catastrophe for her life's work. As she pulled out onto the motorway, she knew she had to call her partner Peter and tell him what she had found. He too would be devastated.

Flyovers and concrete verges flashed past, and as she settled into the easy rhythm of her journey home, she pondered the years since she and Peter had started university together: the late-night discussions, the thesis choices, the patient manipulation of their careers as they worked steadily towards their shared goals. They had wanted to rationalise the way society managed psychology, psychiatry and mental health; they thought they had succeeded. Now, although their reclassification of psychology and their basic diagnosis processes were successful, it looked like the practical application of their work remained flawed and in need of reconsideration. It was disheartening. Proving the need for further improvements to their many investors would be a struggle. That they would also need to challenge how the National Health Service and government were using the results of their analysis: that was most daunting of all. Bev sighed, knowing she was procrastinating, and kicked off a call to Peter. He answered within three rings, surprising for a Sunday morning.

"Bev, hi! How did you get on with Munro? Did you get to the bottom of it all?" he asked immediately, ditching the preliminaries in his eagerness for an update. They had last spoken late on Friday evening, when Bev still harboured some hope that their team had not mis-diagnosed Lana Knight - then wrongly pursued her.

"Peter, I'm afraid it's not good news. Munro was right, there is absolutely nothing wrong with Lana Knight." She paused for a moment to let the news settle in. "I've debriefed her thoroughly, and I have some real concerns about how we've implemented the process at the new clinic – and goodness knows what might be happening where we've handed oversight to others. I think I know how to remedy the situation, but we'll need to halt analysis until we have it sorted. I'm sorry, I know this is the last thing we need..."

Bev was massively relieved when Peter interrupted her, "No, we have no choice. We can flag up our concerns to the other countries who have also picked up the factorisation analysis process; we can get that kicked off immediately. Did you find out what was happening with the Central Care team? Why were they suddenly pursuing an enforced compulsory treatment order?"

Bev sighed. "Pete, I'm on the road. Are you at home? Can I stop in and run through it all with you? I'm too tired to talk and drive, I've been up half the night worrying." As Peter agreed to cancel his plans for the day, Bev was appreciative but still felt an upswell of bitter disappointment. "I managed to keep a brave face in front of Munro, but this is a real mess, Pete. I can sort out the situation for Lana, but we're going to have so much to do before we can restart the analysis. I honestly thought we'd been so careful." Bev stopped before she became any more upset, knowing she needed to stay focused on the road.

"I know," Peter reassured her, "but we'll fix this. It's a good thing that we've found these flaws in the early stages of the changed process. Wait and tell me all about it when you get here. Try not to worry too much." He rang off, leaving Bev with her thoughts and the shushing white noise of tyres on tarmac. Rolling hills and farmland passed in a blur as she traversed the central belt on her journey home.

Peter lived in the heart of Edinburgh, in the lower half of a villa near Murrayfield, which boasted the grandeur and gardens so many estate agents adore. As Bev parked up outside, the noise from the main road barely intruded through the small but dense wooded area which shielded the much quieter street. She had always loved this part of town, but now preferred the convenience of a newer property; high ceilings, draughty windows and crumbling plaster were too much work for her. Her home was in a newer building further from the city centre, where she could walk out to Cramond Island and breathe fresh air straight from the North Sea.

Peter welcomed her, and they headed into his stark, modern, kitchen dining room, the smell of the coffee he had prepared succour to the soul. Bev hopped up onto a comfortably worn leather bar stool, aware of her feet dangling like a child's, and waved her notes from the previous day as Peter filled her mug. In the background, she could hear children playing in their garden, laughter softening their shrieking.

"We can run through everything, but to summarise: I think I know where we've gone wrong. The basics are all good – the testing, the brain scans. We've proved those over and over; thankfully we won't need to hand back any awards," she laughed bitterly. "The models we've used to roll out analysis in other countries, with testing being done over a longer period, and combined with traditional therapies - they will not be as badly affected. But here in the UK, when we chose to condense the testing and analysis into two to three days - it's too much for the patient. They're exhausted, desperate to get home – some people will always take the path of least resistance, say anything just to complete the analysis. And in Lana's case, we've sadly proven that the testing itself is lacking. She was shown the usual three movies to monitor her emotional reactions, but two of those were films she was already incredibly familiar with. Her responses measured as beyond acceptable parameters, but only because they were muted by that familiarity and her own exhaustion. That will be a problem across all test centres globally. Lastly - I hate to say this, but we need to be more careful who we have doing the final analysis, diagnosis and prescribing." She sighed, shook her head. "It always comes down to human factors and second opinions, doesn't it?" She took a breath before continuing. "Lana's analysis was performed by Martha Meziani and Neil Fagan." Peter raised his eyebrows. "I know, in hindsight I should have made sure they weren't paired, but how do I make those rules without looking either biased or prejudiced?" Neil Fagan was an excellent psychologist but inherently cautious, and Martha Meziani had become increasingly fearful since her young child's birth. It was something they were supporting her through, but Bev now feared it was affecting her clinical judgement.

Peter nodded and summarised. "The testing was flawed because of her familiarity with the material, the scans therefore showed concerning reactions to the stimuli, our factorisation algorithms show her as having areas of concern. Plus, she was exhausted by the in-patient process and didn't present well. So, our two most cautious clinical team members... did what, exactly?"

Bev stilled herself before answering, knowing that this was the crux of their problems, wanting nothing more than for it all to be somehow untrue - but aware that denial was of no use to them.

"They prescribed anti-psychotics and anti-depressants; a regime more suitable for someone presenting with serious problems. And unbelievably, they also prescribed the contraceptive pill without discussing that decision with her. Central Care take over all the long-term prescribing and management of repeat meds - that's standard process – so when Martha and Neil had marked it as necessary, they took that as gospel. Lana's GP, Maria Gillies, spotted the contraceptive prescription and advised her to stop taking it, assuming it was an error. They started an appeal to have it removed from her therapy, but their request was refused on the basis that it was part of the planned treatment and not an error. When Lana's medical review showed that she wasn't taking all her necessary medications, the new Central Care authority started trying to enforce compliance. And this is where it's really gone awry! Because our patients sign our legal agreement saying they will accept our findings and all treatments, Central Care used that as a loophole to circumvent the standard process for compulsory treatment orders. Instead of going to a mental health tribunal for review and agreement, they went straight to enforcement. First, they flagged her as a danger to the public, then they informed her employer and she lost her job, then finally they involved the police to bring her into a mental health facility."

Disbelief and horror were marring Peter's usually cheerful face, but Bev pushed on. "Central Care have taken our legal agreement and used it to thwart the patients' rights to representation and fair say. From Lana's point of view, they were trying to commit her for refusing the contraceptives; despite the GP trying their best, she got no opportunity to discuss her treatment after she left our clinic. She could have been forced into care, Pete. For no good reason at all." Bev's eyes were wide with anxiety as she looked at her partner. "And the worst thing is, we only found out about this because we were students with Munro, and he's fallen in love with Lana. This could potentially have happened to other people: lives ruined because of our analysis."

Peter nodded slowly, then winced as a child outside screamed in either anger or pain. No pleasant peace in the unseasonal sunshine for that family. He scrubbed his face with both hands, then sighed. "So tomorrow we call a temporary halt while we work on the issues with the process. You'll clear Lana Knight's record?" he checked. As Bev nodded, he continued, "We'll get the whole team into the clinic, explain it all. We can kick off a review of all the patients we've tested as well; thankfully it's still early days in the UK, Edinburgh has seen less than thirty patients to date. Are you okay to coordinate all of that while I handle the investors and the other European clinics? They've all been using the original model of longer-term testing alongside traditional therapies, so we shouldn't have such an issue there – but we should have them check their patients and prepare to change the testing so familiar video material isn't used." Bev again nodded, this time gratefully; Peter was far more of a people person than she was and would handle the discussions diplomatically. "We'll need to see what's happening at Central Care as well," he concluded.

"I think we should talk to Lana's GP, Maria Gillies," Bev replied. "She's already started investigating and discussing this with the GP Committee and communities. We can pool our resources, I think."

Peter nodded firmly, "I'll set something up for this week. This will be okay, Bev. It's a bump in the road, but now we know the problem and can tackle it."

Bev wished she felt as confident.

Chapter 2 – Monday 17th November

Early morning found Bev at her desk in the Edinburgh clinic, double checking her work to clear Lana Knight's record of concern flags and inappropriate prescriptions. Outside, it was a typical day for late autumn in Scotland: cold, dark, windy and damp. Despite the lights in her cluttered but homely office, there was a persistent gloom she hadn't been able to disperse. She felt it deep in her bones. Attempting to cheer herself up, she had texted Munro to advise Lana was now in the clear, knowing he would worry until he heard. The couple had headed home the day before, but Lana had sensibly decided to stay indoors until there was no chance of her being apprehended. Munro was a natural worrier, made worse by the death of his wife; he would need to learn to give Lana space now that her crisis was past. She seemed a competent and independent person, and certainly not as helpless as Munro seemed to think. Their relationship would need to adjust. Bev was roused from her reverie as Peter entered, and she noted the rumpled features, bleary eyes and drawn forehead of a late night. He had brought her favourite coffee, though, so she decided against teasing him.

"Are you okay? You look like you'd rather be in bed,"

she ventured.

"Mmf. Nothing that isn't my own fault: I was obsessing until the early hours. I'll be fine once I've had this." Peter swished his coffee in his cup and slumped into her guest chair. Bev could understand his sleepless night, she had drifted off easily after her tiring weekend, but had woken at four in the morning, her mind racing and unable to rest any longer. "What time are they all in?" he asked, tilting his head towards the rest of the complex.

"Ten," Bev confirmed grimly. "I worded it as an all-hands; they'll be curious but hopefully not too worried. Will you be up to it?" Peter nodded, and she pushed concern for him to the back of her mind; he had operated on minimal sleep countless times before, and she trusted his judgement.

By ten o'clock, the full team were assembled in the canteen, the only room large enough to hold them all. Most held hot drinks, and a plate of biscuits was slowly being depleted. Bev and Peter stood together at the front of the crowd, drawing strength from each other. This announcement would be a shock and disappointment to everyone here, but as clinicians they would understand the need for the steps they were taking. Even so, it would need to be handled diplomatically, and Bev was glad Peter would do most of the speaking. Her role was to watch for reactions and follow up with anyone who looked to disagree.

Peter started without preamble. "So, we have some news. Bev and I have postponed this week's in-patients; we have called a temporary halt to our analysis programme. I know this comes as a shock to you all, but we have good reason to believe we need a rethink of the logistics of our analysis. Not the testing or technology, but the way we are conducting it here." There was a brief flurry of muttering, rapidly quelled when Peter moved on to explain the situation. Bev watched the faces and body language of their colleagues closely, seeing nothing untoward as Peter detailed their main worries about how the process was currently being facilitated. However, as he brought the specifics of Lana's case to light, the two doctors most heavily involved started to share glances, and Dr Fagan, in particular, looked indignant for a time before he blanked his expression. As their colleagues expressed their horror at how their factorisation profiling had ended, both Meziani and Fagan kept quiet, their eyes to the floor.

"We have already remedied the situation Ms Knight has suffered," Peter continued, "but our most urgent need is for a review of our other test patients. Bev will be leading this, and we shall start work on it today. I will be focused on highlighting our concerns to the other teams who are using our processes. Once we have fresh confidence in all our results, we will move on to adapting how we run the testing and analysis process here, then restart the pilot with the postponed patient list. Bev and I will lead the process redesign, obviously, but we will be involving some of you throughout. Bev will also be responsible for discussions with Central Care about their processes once they have a patient's results and therapy plan."

Bev watched the team set aside their shock and move on to the practicalities of the next few weeks, feeling a warm pride at their pragmatism and resilient professionalism. As Peter asked for questions and the discussion delved into details, she noted that neither Fagan nor Meziani were engaging with him. Sighing, she resigned herself to a longer discussion with them.

Neil Fagan was an easily forgettable man, of average build and features, and quiet nature. He was an excellent observer of people, his unobtrusive character giving his patients the much-needed space to be themselves. He was generally calm, and with nearly twenty years of experience he rarely showed his emotions at work. Usually highly competent, Bev had noticed a more jaded aspect to him in the last few months but had written it off to personal issues. Now she wondered if there had been a deeper problem and regretted not having enquired. He sat directly across from Bev, a tremor playing in his hands and uncertainty clear upon his face.

"I don't understand. The test results were very clear. We simply wrote them up and prescribed according to the protocols," he explained to Bev's dismay. Martha Meziani nodded fervently beside him.

"Yes," Bev accepted before countering, "but that isn't what we're meant to do. The test results are not gospel, they should always be tempered by our own judgement. That is why the results are analysed by at least two clinicians who have also spent time in talking therapy with the patient." Bev again explained her theory of the correlation between a patient's familiarity with the video being shown, muted emotional responses, and skewed results from their scans. "When the results so clearly deviated from what we saw in person, we should have done more talking therapy, more testing, until it became clear whether there was an issue or not. It's evident that there is nothing wrong with Lana Knight." Bev refrained from laying the blame squarely at their feet, knowing that hindsight made for easy targets. In truth, she should have been more cautious with the changes to the testing, and it was her responsibility. "We'll need to make that very clear as part of the revised process."

"And you're absolutely sure that Lana Knight doesn't present any concerning symptoms?" Martha persisted. Bev took in her clutched hands and hunched shoulders, knowing that her colleague was stressed and anxious on most good days, and would take careful handling.

"Absolutely. She was under immense stress when I saw her - but coping admirably without any indication she was mentally unwell. This is absolutely the processes at fault," she emphasized, hoping that it would sink in.

"I don't understand why she was referred if she wasn't unwell," Neil persisted, clearly wanting to be rid of any responsibility he might carry.

Bev sighed. "She was concerned, but it's clear now that she was over-worrying about some fairly normal feelings. She hadn't been for any of the usual therapies, this was her first visit to her GP about it. Because I knew her GP, she seemed a good candidate for the pilot, but that was my mistake. No matter whether she should have been tested, however, it should always be the case that a mentally healthy person would be able to undergo our testing and not be misdiagnosed. Under the circumstances we currently use, that isn't the case: we should focus on how we improve the process."

Bev understood why they were both being defensive: their peers would know it was their patient case which had gone wrong. But she was also reluctant to completely absolve them of blame; they had at the very least been too reliant on the testing and hadn't done their own due diligence. However, she let them leave and join the team reviewing the patient case list, hoping she wouldn't have to argue that point again.

Glancing at the clock, she realised she had only twenty minutes until the call Peter had set up with Maria Gillies; she should grab a coffee while there was time. As her stomach rumbled, and fatigue nagged at her coordination, she realised she hadn't yet eaten and decided to pick up an early lunch while she was there. As she hurried to the canteen, she saw Martha and Neil huddled against the wind in the central courtyard, and her heart sank: they clearly weren't happy. She would have Peter talk to them later.

Peter closed the door to Bev's office and pulled a chair up to her desk, preferring to be in the room with at least one person rather than joining the call alone from his desk. Bev knew he preferred to meet people in person, but these days video calls were very much the norm; a half day away from the clinic for a thirty-minute meeting would be a rare indulgence. But video calls seemed to squash Peter's natural exuberance and charm, and she suspected he missed having those advantages, rather than harbouring the usual usability concerns about lag and distortion.

As they waited for the others to join, Bev reprised the attendee list. "Maria has forwarded on the invite to Tom Brightman, he's the Scottish chair of the GP Committee. They know each other reasonably well, and he's already up to speed. She didn't invite Lana's solicitor, to save her fees; hopefully his services won't be needed any longer, so she said she would email him a brief update and leave it to Lana to deal with him after that."

Peter nodded, frowning slightly. "I wonder if Tom Brightman has contacts at Central Care?"

Bev shrugged, about to speak when they were notified of the others joining. Straightening her back, she started the call. This was the first time she had seen Maria Gillies, and she was surprised to find that the stern, serious GP had an open, amenable face and close-cropped silver hair which had been highlighted with rose gold hints. Maria smiled broadly at Bev and Peter, starting the discussion by thanking Bev for her help with Lana Knight. She moved immediately to introduce the fourth attendee.

"This is Tom, he's a senior partner at a practice in Glasgow and chairs the Scottish branch of the BMA's GP Committee. I've already raised my concerns with them as well as with the local GP community groups and online forums. Tom has been nominated to take our concerns forward."

As Bev and Peter nodded, Tom took over. "Thank you for your time this morning. And I'll second Maria's thanks to you for clearing the patient's record. I know you'll both have concerns regarding your analysis programme: we want to ensure patients continue seeing the benefit of the new factorisation, while resolving any issues. But the GPC's most pressing concern is the introduction of your new legal agreements, and the precedent that has been set in Lana's case."

Peter was already nodding. "Yes, we agree; the other issues we can handle internally. Our legal agreements were introduced purely because this is a new analysis process, and we wanted to ensure that the effort wasn't being wasted. The patient agrees to take part in the full process, including any ongoing therapies and re-testing. They commit to attend the results meeting, where they agree any required medication or treatment with the clinicians. They commit to following through on those treatment plans, including the meds. I can send you both a copy of the standard agreement." Both Maria and Tom nodded their thanks. "Neither of us," here Peter glanced at Bev, who was staring intently at her hands, "ever expected our legal agreement to be used by Central Care; a signed copy is loaded into the patient record, but only for information. When we heard it was being used to try and enforce care, we were stunned."

Tom raised an eyebrow. "That's an understatement!" he pronounced. "We see this as Central Care firmly outstepping the bounds of their remit. We'll be taking this up with them and the Scottish government as well as the wider NHS authorities: my counterparts in England and Wales are on side. I imagine we will need you to explain the situation and support our arguments. Will that be possible?"

As Bev and Peter agreed, Maria Gillies spoke up once more. "I'll be happy to represent Ms Knight in all this if needed - although I expect she may have to testify as well. What sort of timeframe are we looking at, Tom?"

The chair considered this for a moment. "I'll start chasing this up immediately, but I suspect it will be early next year before we can get any traction and start discussing things properly. How much time will your team need to work through your concerns?" he asked Peter.

Peter turned to Bev: this was her domain. "We can be in a good position by the end of this year, I think," she estimated. "By then we'll have reviewed all our results, checked in with patients, and have a formal plan for restarting the analysis. It ought to tie in quite well with your timeframes; we shouldn't have any loose ends left when you bring this up for discussion."

As they finalised their plan for the next two months,

Bev found herself relieved to hand over the considerable responsibility for liaising with Central Care and the government; she would have her hands full as it was. She glanced once again at the clock, realising it was nearly one. The day was passing so quickly, and she had so much to do. She would prioritise getting involved with the patient record reviews this afternoon, then this evening she would head home for a light supper followed by a hot bath and an ice-cold gin and tonic, her favourite treat. Tomorrow was a fresh day, and she resolved to be better prepared for it than she had been for today.

Chapter 3 – Saturday 27th December

Lana was staying with her parents, having temporarily given use of her flat to her sister and baby nephew until they were able to buy their own home. She had packed most of her clothes into boxes and stashed them in her parent's attic, but now for the first time she wished she had her full wardrobe to browse: she had no idea what to wear to lunch with Bev and Peter. She had an hour to prepare before they headed off to meet them, so she decided to postpone the decision to the last minute.

As she headed into the kitchen, she called through to her mother, offering her a cup of tea. She smiled as she heard her gather her crutches: her mum still preferred to get things herself despite the debilitating effects of the multiple sclerosis which tormented her. They sat down together at the table, and Lana smiled. An unexpected benefit of being home for a few weeks was the refreshed friendship she now shared with her mum, having been closer to her dad since her teenage years.

"When's Munro picking you up?" her mum asked, taking a minute sip of too-hot tea as she eyed Lana's loungewear.

"One," she replied. "We're heading down into Fife to meet them, save either of us driving all the way. I'm a bit nervous, to be honest – which is mad considering I've already met Bev and spent a weekend with her." Her mum had no chance to answer before she continued, "I guess it's just different today because we're meeting under such normal circumstances - well, almost humdrum really! I don't have any excuse for being a mess this time," she laughed.

"That's understandable," her mum agreed. "But I bet none of them would want you nervous. I'd wear layers," she added, getting to the heart of the immediate problem. "Old pubs can be either freezing or roasting depending on whether your table is at the door or the fire."

The drive through Fife was spectacular, the low sun gleaming off bare tree limbs dripping with melted frost. Peter lounged in the passenger side, playing with the heated seat controls and hopping through radio stations. Bev was used to this restlessness: he wasn't someone built to be constrained. He tutted as they slowed through the traffic calming measures installed in every village and town, keen to get to the pub they had chosen; he'd not eaten since early morning and had grumbled off and on about the late Sunday lunch since Bev picked him up.

"So, what's Lana like, really?" he asked. "It's weird to know so much about someone without having met them."

Bev grinned. "She's younger than us; beautiful. She certainly seems intelligent, and strikes me as being quite independent and competent, too. She was surprisingly logical and calm, given everything she had been going through." Bev thought for a moment, trying to summarise her impression of Lana from both the testing at the clinic and the impromptu overnight they had shared at Munro's cottage. "I think she's quite a confident, grounded person most of the time, but insecure about her emotional side. Very practical and creative, you should have seen the tea tray thing she had made from some old tat Munro had lying around."

"I honestly didn't think he would meet anyone else," Peter mused. "After Ann died, it was like he'd aged forty years."

Bev tilted her head in agreement. "It seems to have been a bit of a whirlwind thing. I suspect he's in for a shock, though – he was acting like she's some weak damsel in distress, but I think she's more than capable of looking after herself. It'll be interesting to see how they get on. It's a good sign that they're bringing Stuart with them today, we'll see how she handles a future stepson." Bev raised her eyebrows, and they shared a smile: one thing they had always agreed on was that children were for other people, not them.

"That reminds me, I didn't ask if you had seen your family this year, in the end?" Peter asked. Bev was the older sister of four brothers, all of whom had married and had children. They were now scattered throughout England and Scotland, but every second Christmas the whole family congregated back at their parent's country home for a few days. This year, Bev had been due to join them, but at the last minute she had chosen to stay in Edinburgh to work; it hadn't proven popular with her parents.

"I stayed here and completed the reviews," she admitted. "I wanted to start the new year with that behind us... but in all honesty I wasn't really looking forward to the latest round of "Who's earned most?"" she grimaced.

"They've all become so materially competitive; it's bizarre. Rob is the only one whose wife still works, but despite her loving her career, he's always pushing her to give it up because the others use their homemaker wives as some sort of bizarre retro status symbol. It gives me the pip," she finally declared.

Peter was familiar with Bev's family and the strain she carried whenever she saw them: she just couldn't reconcile the men they had become with the younger brothers she had adored as a girl. Peter was an only child from a modest background but felt no envy for her large family, generous but strict parents, and ancient and rambling farmhouse home. She had gone out of her way to deliberately avoid their archetypal bucolic family Christmas, the likes of which dominated Hollywood Christmas films, while he had been infinitely happier spending his Christmas Day alone with his parents in their tiny bungalow.

As they pulled into the carpark, Bev recognised Munro's car and slotted into the space alongside, smiling as Peter launched himself out of the car before she had even released her seatbelt. As they walked to the entrance, Bev looked out over wintery fields and bright skies dominated by the low sun, glad they had come out of the city for the day. The clinic was officially closed over the Christmas break, but Bev had been working long hours every day and the change of terrain cheered her. She needed a break as much as everyone else, and she resolved to stop working for a few days until after New Year.

Peter was already at their table as she entered, introducing himself to Lana and teasing Stuart about how much he had grown since they last met. Bev was amused to see Stuart look to his dad nervously; clearly, he had forgotten Peter entirely. She smiled as she joined them.

"Don't worry about him, Stuart, he thinks everyone should remember him even if they've only met him once for five minutes. Oh, I'm glad we got a table near the fire, I always seem to be chilly nowadays." She glanced at Lana, who had already shed her cardigan and was still rosy-cheeked, envying her.

As they sat down and caught up, Bev watched Lana with Stuart as she helped him read the menu and choose his dishes, pleased to see them so relaxed in each other's company. When she offered to swap her plate with his if he didn't like the sea bass he was considering, her liking for the younger woman was cemented. Munro caught her eye, obviously aware of her thoughts, and she smiled her approval.

The meal was relaxed and festive, the clinicians swapping stories of their medical school days, and Lana getting to know them all a little better. The log fire snapped and sizzled beside them as new logs were added to the blaze, and the weak sunlight filtering through the small-paned windows glinted on the Christmas decorations around them. Stuart thrived on the attention Peter lavished on him, sharing his tablet and the latest games he was enjoying. As they finished their desserts, he immersed himself in a video, and Munro turned to Bev.

"So," he dissembled, "how's your work going?"

Bev smiled, understanding the need for caution. "We're getting there. It's been a bit of a slog, but we've completed our reviews and now we're working on the new process. Thankfully we didn't get any pushback from the senior administrators, they understood the need to stop and assess."

Lana was frowning slightly. "Do you have any better idea of what you might need from me?" she asked, checking Stuart wasn't paying attention. But Bev was shaking her head and shrugging, so she changed tack. "No worries, there's no rush. I don't have any big plans coming up. We were thinking of heading down to the cottage at Easter, but if you need me for anything I can always travel from there. I'm desperate from a proper rummage through the old furniture in the store," she admitted with a laugh. "Did Munro tell you I'd started selling some pieces? I pick things up at auctions and on selling sites, give them a refresh, then sell them on my own online store. It's been slow going so far, as I build up stock, but I'm already starting to get interest locally from people who want their own old pieces renovated. It looks quite promising. I'm working out of my dad's garage for now, so there are no real overheads. Eventually I'll need to get a bigger space to store and sell completed items; Munro wants me to think about using the big garage at his house, but I'm tempted to try and find someplace with more footfall. There's only so much business word of mouth will generate."

"Bev told me you'd revamped some of Munro's furniture at the cottage, how nice it was," Peter mentioned. "Do you have any photos?"

Lana showed him some of her work, explaining how she was trying to build a mixed stock of larger and smaller pieces so there was always something affordable to tempt window-shoppers, occasionally explaining how she had changed the pieces from damaged and dated to something more modern. Munro watched, pride and admiration clear in his eyes. It was clear that they were deeply in love, and that would get them past the stressful and unconventional start to their relationship. Bev smiled to herself, enjoying the Christmas spirit for the first time that year.

Chapter 4 – Tuesday 6th January

Munro closed the fridge door with a knee and juggled his way over to the chopping board, nearly losing his grip on a red pepper. Stuart was in his room, immersed in his miniature robot toys, and their childminder, Laurie, had already headed for home. It was rare that he had the kitchen to himself, and he briefly revelled in the freedom, knowing that soon he would be joined by his son and subject to a world of questions. As he started to chop onions, mushrooms and peppers, he heated their large cast iron skillet and mentally ran through the spices he would need for their chicken fajitas. Lana often ate with them nowadays, but they were keen to return Stuart to a more normal routine before he went back to school, so tonight they were on their own and could eat messily. Fajitas were one of Stuart's favourites, but he had yet to learn how to wrap the filling securely and was nervous of dropping it all in company. He was checking the temperature of the pan, just about to start cooking, when his phone rang.

Lana was scrubbing her hands: despite wearing gloves she always seemed to get paint somewhere unexpected.

Tonight, her dad was cooking, so she had lingered an extra hour finishing a coat of paint on a dressing table which reminded her of her old dolls-house furniture. It was a commission for a friend of a friend; the owner ran a boutique hotel, so Lana was keen to make a good impression. The dressing table and matching stool were incredibly careworn when they arrived; after repairing the damaged wood she was now working to make them a smooth and glossy midnight blue, with deep indigo velvet upholstery on the stool. As she dried her hands and started visually checking the garage was squared away for the night, her phone rang.

Bev was hunched over her desk, head, neck and back aching, studying the latest data from their process trials; searching for anomalies which might hint at the sort of problems they had seen in Lana's case. She knew that anxiety and uncertainty were driving her to over-work, and that if she was too tired, she wouldn't be at her best, but each day she still struggled to leave before she was entirely exhausted. She was rubbing the heels of her hands into her eyes when she was jolted by a shout from down the corridor. She rushed out to the canteen, where Peter was watching the TV on the wall, frantically increasing the volume.

A newsreader faced the camera sternly. "Tonight, we have learned that the celebrated Psychological Factorisation programme of testing has been halted, in the midst of allegations of erroneous results. As far back as November, patients have had their scheduled appointments cancelled or postponed, and allegations have been made that some patients may have been wrongly diagnosed and treated. It is unclear at this time how many have been affected, or who they may be. Psychological Factorisation is now being used across Europe, and its British creators were the recipients of a Nobel Prize a little over a year ago. Our correspondent is in Edinburgh, where the testing has been being piloted in the UK."

Bev looked at Peter in disbelief as she recognised the carpark outside their clinic, the reporter standing in wind and rain outside their doors. As the storm-tossed woman gradually admitted to having no more information for the viewers, Bev sank into a plastic chair, shaking her head in disbelief.

Peter came to sit beside her, as shaken as she was. "I mean, we haven't been keeping it secret, but... Why on earth are the BBC reporting on it? Who has spoken to them about it? Why wouldn't they clarify that no one has been hurt or anything? Why would anyone make this much fuss about a clinical process?"

"It must be a quiet news day," Bev initially guessed, before shaking her head again. "No, no. This is sensationalist news, isn't it? It all sounds terrifying, the way they've worded it. This new testing - which already has some fear factor because of the new technologies and categorical results - now it turns out that it can go wrong? They're scare mongering. What a nightmare." She turned to Peter, aghast. "I'm surprised our phones aren't ringing already."

"They must have wanted a scoop – other journalists will be on the case shortly, I imagine. We already have the wording we used to explain the halt to the NHS administrators, we can re-purpose that as an official statement. I'll update it to explain where we are with the results and when we expect to restart testing. Don't worry, it'll blow over when they realise that the testing isn't particularly faulty."

"But what if they ever find out that Central Care tried to enforce treatment on someone as a result of our testing? The press will go mad," Bev countered.

But Peter was shaking his head. "No, that would be breaking patient confidentiality. Don't worry. And that was Central, not us or our testing."

Bev laughed, knowing she sounded mildly hysterical and not caring. "It's the British media, Peter. They won't care who was responsible. If they find out anything about it, they'll make the most of it without caring about the effect on our patients or our team. I'd better warn Lana: hopefully they won't get anywhere near her, but she should know." As she turned back towards her office to make the call, both their office phones started to ring.

Rain still drummed against the clinic doors as Bev left later that night. Peter had headed home an hour before, but Bev had remained, resting her eyes and head in the comfortable quiet of her office before she tackled the drive home. They had called Lana and Munro, letting them know of the developments, then emailed their team. Bev had been interested to note that Martha Meziani had read and responded to the email immediately, declaring that she thought it best that the public knew what had been happening. Bev suspected that she was still feeling defensive and at odds with the rest of the team and made a note to speak with her again soon.

As she crossed the deserted city streets, and approached her home, her tension eased somewhat. The clinic was too public, too accessible to journalists. Even at this late hour, she had worried that she may be asked for her thoughts before Peter had a chance to make his formal statement. She was glad that worry was behind her. Exhausted, shedding her damp clothes and climbing into bed, she was grateful for the solitude and predictability of living alone.

The next morning rose bright and clear, a blessing after the torrents of rain the day before. Resigned to a fraught day, Bev retraced her journey from a mere 7 hours before, wondering how her team would react to having the scrutiny of the media upon them. Often, she stopped and picked up treats for everyone to share, but today she rejected the notion, worrying that it would seem like an appeasement. As she entered their part of the hospital, however, she was pleased to find her staff relaxed and hard at work: she had underestimated them. Peter was there before her, again surprising her.

"We've already discussed it all to death," he admitted. "We're as prepared as we can be, and I've arranged to make our formal statement at 10. I asked everyone just to carry on with their agreed workloads for now," he concluded.

Gratitude welled in Bev, both for Peter's professionalism and for the level-headedness of their colleagues; now she realised she was over-worrying and catastrophising and regretted her decision to swerve the local bakery. She would pick up something at lunchtime.

Chapter 5 – Thursday 8th January

The deep tones of a large dog barking reverberated through the hall, borne in from the street by a brisk wind which still retained the frosted salt freshness of the North Sea. Lana heeled shut the heavy front door behind her and struggled out of her boots, scarf and coat. Untangling the handles of the shopping bags she bore, she headed through the smartly tiled hall and into the brightly lit kitchen. Counters were covered in flour and discarded ingredients, and a pot simmered aromatically on the polished glass hob. Munro and Stuart both looked up at the same time, and their expressions were so perfectly matched in their happiness to see her that Lana stopped short, letting loose a surprised giggle. Sudden emotion warmed her cold hands and face.

"You two look like you're making good progress!" she exclaimed. "I picked up the Parma ham, a jar of artichokes, and some fresh basil, but they didn't have any salami left, sorry," she explained, unpacking her first bag. "They did have a rather nice-looking cream sponge for after, though," she added, putting the rest of her groceries directly into the fridge and cupboards to avoid getting in their way. This was pizza night, and she knew not to offer to help, so she set the dining table and poured drinks for them all.

"How did the casting of the play go, Stuart?" she asked, as they all worked. Stuart had been hoping to be given the role of Robin Hood in his school's medieval extravaganza, and they had all been a little on tenterhooks about the announcement. Munro's eyebrows raised but he otherwise gave no hints as to the outcome.

"I didn't get Robin Hood," Stuart answered. "Justin got it, but he'll make a really good one, so it's okay. I'm going to be the narrator, and that means I have the most lines to learn and the most difficult job," he continued. "Only I could be trusted with it!" he added with a proud grin.

"Oh, wow, that sounds even better than Robin," Lana replied, worrying briefly that she was overdoing her reaction. "Will you still get to dress up?"

"Oh, yes, I'm going to be dressed like a merchant, with a scroll to read from, but not all my words will be on it, so I still need to learn all my lines off by heart."

Lana couldn't help but be charmed by this boy she had only known for a few weeks. He was so cheerful, and thankful, and so much like his father in his nature. She had worried about meeting Munro's son, fretting that she wasn't used to children, that she wouldn't know how to talk to him, that he might not like having to share his dad with her. But he had surprised them both, taking to her immediately and welcoming her into his life openly – much like he took to everything else, she had later discovered. He was an easy-going, happy kid with a generous heart. She knew how lucky she was, having heard horror stories of other children reacting badly to their parents' new partners and ruining the chances of them ever getting along as they'd hoped. But it went farther than that, she realised. He was simply easily lovable, and she was really very fond of him already. It was a little revelation to her, and she busied herself for a while to cover her surprise.

As they ate the delicious pizzas, and chatted over their days, there was a calm normality to their interactions, very different from their nervy, giggly, more strained, early meetings. She caught Munro's eye, and he smiled warmly at her, perhaps sharing her thoughts. This new life may have been unexpected, a complete departure from what she may have expected a year or so before - but for that she appreciated it all the more.

Later, once Stuart was in bed and they had settled into the sofa for the evening, they made sure to catch the late news. Today, Bev and Peter had been expecting a statement from the Scottish government, giving their thoughts on the halting of their testing. Lana and Munro were anxious to hear it. Finally, the newsreader turned their attention to the story.

"Today, the Scottish government has committed to investigate the failings of the Bryant Cargill Psychological Factorisation programme. The lauded analysis, which has been temporarily halted following reports of the misdiagnosis of at least one patient, is still on hold. It is unknown at this time what the extent of the programme's failings may be, however in a statement by the lead clinicians it has been made clear that all patients negatively affected by the programme have been contacted. They have also confirmed that testing will remain on hold until all contributing factors have been reviewed and, if needed, remedied. The First Minister stated that a committee would be immediately convened to determine the full facts behind the matter, and to consider the future direction of any such analysis undertaken by NHS Scotland. They also committed to uncovering whether any confidential patient information had been mishandled at any time. A source close to the Bryant Cargill team has confirmed that they will be represented on the committee, as will at least one former patient. The UK government has stated only that this is an internal issue for NHS Scotland and the Scottish government, and that they are not involved at this time."

As the newsreader moved on, Munro breathed a low whistle while lowering the volume. Lana widened her eyes in response.

"It's so odd, seeing something that happened to me on the news," she offered, knowing words couldn't express the full extent of her feelings.

Munro nodded, stroking the back of her hand with his thumb. "It could have been worse, I guess – it was quite a calm report. I'm not sure the rest of the media will be quite as considered. I haven't heard from Bev today, but I know that she's been involved in the organisation of the committee – in fact, she and others from NHS Scotland have been leading it, not the government. But I guess they would spin it that way, try and take the lead from a political standpoint."

"Ugh, politics," Lana grimaced. "They'd turn everything on its head to make sure they don't come out looking bad," she posited. "Thank God Bev is in charge. I wonder when she'll need me to talk to them?" she pondered.

"I wish you didn't need to do that," Munro worried. "I hate that you'll be in the media's eye. I worry what they'll say: whether they'll make everything sound awful."

Lana raised an eyebrow, not entirely sure what he was alluding to. "They can try to make me look awful, but that would mean the testing was right all along, surely?" she joked. "Or they could try to make us all look bad or incompetent, but Bev and Peter have already been totally honest about the shortcomings they've found: what else could they complain about?"

Munro looked unconvinced but shook off his concerns. "So long as you're sure you're happy to do this?" he asked.

Lana nodded firmly. "At the moment, they're all focused on what might have gone wrong in the testing, and the after-effects of that. What they should really be worried about is that it's fundamentally wrong to commit a patient to care on the word of one set of results or opinions. This committee needs to see and understand that, make changes to ensure that never happens, no matter what transpires with the factorisation analysis." She sighed. "Let's not talk about it anymore tonight, I get so tired of it all," she admitted.

They relaxed, chatting on and off, holding each other and finding comfort in intimacy. Lana finally sighed. "I should really go; let you get to bed. I know Stuart is an early riser."

Munro thumped his head back into the soft sofa. "I wish you didn't have to leave. I know it's selfish of me, and I know we agreed we'd wait before springing 'sleepovers' on Stuart, but I still wish you could stay here, even just some of the time. Stealing moments alone together is for teenagers, not men my age," he griped. "I know, I know, I'm being as grumpy as a teenager right now," he laughed self-consciously, shaking his head.

Lana smiled, agreeing with him but also knowing he

wouldn't seriously consider rushing Stuart into a new situation. "A few more weeks, and he'll be going down to stay with your parents for the in-service days. We'll have the house to ourselves then. And it's better to take things at the right pace for him. We'd regret it otherwise."

They took their time saying goodnight before Lana left, heading out into calmer conditions. The crisp, cold air was fresh in her lungs as she lengthened her stride and headed back towards her parents' home. She smiled as she remembered Munro's consternation on the first occasion that she had made this short walk late at night: he, wanting to make sure she got home safely and frustrated by having to stay home with Stuart; Lana, knowing that she often went out late at night, and not worrying about it at all. There had been a tipping point reached, where he had nearly annoyed her with his concerns and his assumption that she couldn't look after herself despite years of evidence to the contrary. Thankfully, he had realised his error in time, and apologised; he was now careful to make no fuss about these things. She suspected that he still harboured some old-fashioned attitudes, but she was not concerned: he was the smartest person she knew, and so far, he had been happy to let go of old and unnecessary conventions when she pointed out their illogic. The compromise did not all sit with Munro, however: Lana had learned to soften her independence somewhat, knowing how happy it made him to help her. She hoped they were both adapting equally.

While she walked, boots slipping slightly on the frosty pavements, her phone pinged, and she checked her messages in surprise. Who would be in touch at this late hour? But as she saw it was from her friend Lind, she relaxed, no longer worrying that it might be bad news. Lind had been out with their friends, she saw - she had attached a photo of Lana's school friends, Colin and Sanj, leaning in on either side of Lind's happy face. Ailsa was also there, leaning over Colin's shoulder, sticking her tongue out and screwing her eyes shut. The caption read "We miss you! Come out to play sometime!" Lana acknowledged the light rebuke with a wince. The one downside to her new relationship with Munro was that she had less time to spend with her friends, who she loved very much. Lana saw that the group had adapted as she became less available, Lind easily filling the central gap that she had left. She felt a pang of remorse at missing out, before shrugging it off resolutely. There was plenty time for her friends in the coming months, and only a couple of nights of the week when she, Munro and Stuart were all free to spend the evening at their home. She'd made the right choice this time.

Chapter 6 – January

Friday 9th January

Bev furtively checked her appearance as she passed a darkened, reflective storefront window, hoping that she didn't look too much like she had just spent 12 hours at her desk. She would love to say that this was unusual for her, that she normally went home and prepared for a night out, but that just wasn't the case. She hated the fuss of grooming herself, felt no need to impress anyone with her appearance - so gaining a couple of extra hours at work and heading directly to the restaurant seemed smart.

As she trotted around the last corner, glad to see she wasn't too late, she wondered again what tonight would bring. Peter didn't usually introduce his girlfriends to anyone, keeping his private life quietly separate from friendships and workplace. It would be easy to attribute this to the brevity of most of his relationships, but Bev knew better: sadly, Peter had never recovered his ability to trust following a traumatic love affair when he was younger, and he compartmentalised his life to avoid having to reveal that. Today, he had surprised her by asking her to join him for dinner with a new woman in his life.

The welcome at the restaurant door was genuine and radiant, and it buoyed her mood. As she passed the open kitchens and was taken up steep, dark, wood-panelled stairs to the dining area, the aromas of the rich food of old Mumbai enticed her. Peter and Sophie were already at their table, poring over the menu, as she slid into a chair opposite their banquette.

"Hi!" Sophie opened, leaving Peter looking a little uncertain. "I'm Sophie, it's lovely to meet you."

Bev smiled, responding vaguely and trying to work out this new dynamic: Peter was never uncertain. He looked sheepishly at the menu.

"I'd forgotten that so much of this menu was sharing plates," he apologised. "Is that okay with you both?"

"Of course," Bev frowned lightly, "I'm happy to try anything. I love the food here," she explained to Sophie. "I much prefer trying new things, and sharing plates are a lovely way to do that. Are you fond of Indian food, Sophie?" she asked.

As they shared their love of the food here, and the evocative décor, Bev relaxed a little; Sophie seemed pleasant and attractive, and was certainly intelligent and confident – a change from the younger, more flighty characters Peter would occasionally describe. For a long time now, he had avoided anyone who might challenge his ways and habits, preferring to play it safe with impressionable women rather than risk falling for another independent powerhouse, as he had before. Bev privately thought that he prioritised the wrong characteristics in the women he dated, though she held hope for him yet.

The meal passed sociably, and although the two women had little in common bar their taste in food, they both enjoyed their first encounter. Peter, however, remained quiet and pensive. When Sophie excused herself from the table, Bev snatched the opportunity to quiz him.

"So, you were okay when you left the clinic earlier, has something happened? You've been very quiet," she continued.

Peter looked sheepish. "I need to explain. I've only been seeing Sophie for a couple of weeks, but last night I was up late, we were chatting – and she asked what was worrying me. I told her what's been happening," he opened.

"Okay," she shrugged. "Why is that worrying you, though?"

"Sophie is a data protection specialist. She works for a software agency, as a consultant. I mentioned that we think we have a leak in the team, that someone seemed to have gone to the media, and she's a bit concerned. We thought it was best if she had the chance to explain it to you herself: that's why I wanted you to meet her tonight," he detailed.

"Oh, that makes more sense, then," she agreed, before realising she maybe ought not to admit her surprise at the invitation. "Why are you so worried, though?" she deflected.

"Here she is now," was the only answer forthcoming, as he directed his familiar, bright and toothy smile across the tables. "I was just telling Bev that you had some thoughts on our leak," he advised.

"Oh, good. I didn't want to spoil the meal, but I am a little concerned," she sat forward, became far more business-like. "All the staff have access to the patient data, yes?"

"Yes," agreed Bev. "They need it for their roles - that's standard in the NHS. But they're all checked during the hiring process, and everything they view or do is audited in all the systems," she explained.

"Okay," nodded Sophie. "However, one of you," she gestured between Bev and Peter, "would be the data protection officer, and take responsibility for it, yes?"

Bev nodded; it was part of her role.

"I could go into a load of details, but I'm sure you already know the basics, distinctions between data controllers and data processors, and the like." Sophie missed the uncertain look which passed between Bev and Peter. "The main concern I have is that you and the NHS serve as both a data controller and processor. Your leak, your mole? They're processing NHS data on your behalf, but you as DPO have declared which data will be held and what it can and can't be used for, policies to protect confidentiality, etc. If they leak patient data, maliciously or otherwise, you could be held responsible for allowing that to happen, if you haven't been diligent. You need to report data breaches as soon as possible - but if that is then investigated, or if someone sues you, then they can find that you've been negligent. You, personally, as well as the organisation," she reiterated. "It's a bothersome area, especially after we left the EU. And nowadays, often an organisation will attempt to distance itself from whoever they deem responsible for being in charge when the leak happened."

"I see." Bev thought this through. "We already knew all this, though. We've all had the data protection training, and it's all explained whenever new teams or projects are kicked off. I haven't deviated from standard NHS data handling policies." Bev looked to Peter, who nodded.

"Yes," Sophie agreed, "but I'd be worried about what NHS Scotland would do if you do have a breach, especially with the media involved. In most cases, it's cheaper for the organisation to replace the person responsible, attempting to blame them rather than risk having to pay larger fines or more legal fees."

"You think they'd fire me if there was a data breach by one of my staff?" Bev asked her to clarify.

Sophie nodded unhappily. "I've seen it done elsewhere in the last couple of years; precedents have been set, so it's very possible. I don't want to be too alarmist, but you should make sure your back is entirely covered - and find your mole before they leak any patient data."

"No," Bev interjected. "There's no way any of our team would do that. They're all dedicated clinicians, protecting patient confidentiality is second nature to them."

Peter winced in disagreement. "I wouldn't have believed anyone would go to the media about the halting of the testing, but they did. And on last night's news they knew that we – and a patient – would be working with the committee."

"'A source close to...' is what they said. I wonder," Bev mused. "I still don't believe they would leak patient data, though. God, I hope not," she concluded.

"And that's why we were worried," Peter fretted, then sighed. "I think we need some more wine," he concluded.

Tuesday 13th January

"I've got the invite through for the first committee meeting." Bev thumped a coffee mug down onto Peter's desk. "Latte," she grunted, waving her fingers from it to him. "It's not until the end of February! And that's assuming everyone is available, and it isn't postponed," she exclaimed. "Honestly, by the time they convene, and we present our results, and they talk it over for weeks on end... Nothing will be even close to resolved until summer at the earliest! Never mind discussing the greater implications of it all."

She realised she was fretfully pacing the small room, and flopped into a club chair, knocking paperwork off its arm and onto the floor. Her own half-drunk coffee slopped up and dribbled over the rim of her mug, forcing her to stop talking and rescue it.

"We knew that would be the case," Peter ventured.

"Oh, I know," she sighed. "But seeing it in the calendar is just so deflating. We can't restart the testing with our adjustments until after this. Yes, we can do a huge amount of the trialling and prep-work, but it just delays the good we know we can do. I want to get back to working with patients, Pete! And it all looks so bad to the other countries who have been thinking about picking it up. Why did we tinker with it at all, Peter?" Bev spat in frustration and regret. But they both knew that it wasn't just their tinkering with the process which had caused their issues.

"Some of it was flawed in the original process that's been used elsewhere. That would have become apparent eventually in any case," Peter reminded her, gently. "At least everyone has been happy to take our guidance on adapting the process and are moving ahead with that. Their progress will get us some good data to back our case here," he continued, determined to look upon the positives. "Is the invite list being made public?" he returned to the committee meeting.

"Yes. Don't worry, I've warned Lana. Hopefully the media will be distracted by something else and won't pester her about it. Thank God for coffee," she sighed. "Otherwise, I'd never make it through all this."

Thursday 22nd January

Bev rarely considered leaving her work early – in truth, she rarely left until well past when she should have. However, today she could no longer focus; the last few weeks had taken their toll, leaving her overwrought, under-rested, and bad tempered. She looked longingly through her office door and down the corridor, towards the exit. Leaving early would shock her staff; she would need a good excuse if she did decide to make a break for the fresh air.

She was still unresolved when Martha Meziani entered her line of sight and knocked tentatively on her doorframe.

"You wanted to see me yesterday, Bev, but I had to leave early for an appointment. Is now a good time?" she asked.

Bev refocused, turning aside her disappointment at this interruption, and steeled herself: she must not show any tiredness or ill demeanour now.

"Come in, thanks for stopping by," she smiled as best she could. "How are things with you?" She hoped she was expressing a fond interest, but suspected her face was too honest.

"I'm good, thanks. Little Dana is doing well at her new nursery, they're always sending home little bits and pieces of art and the like. I feel much less divided now she's somewhere more reliable."

Martha's toddler daughter had already moved nursery twice, and Bev truly hoped things would work out better for her colleague at this new, very exclusive care centre.

"That's marvellous. I know so many parents who worry themselves sick about childcare; I'm glad it's going well. Everyone says they grow up so quickly, but I imagine that's not the case if you're worrying the whole time when they're young," she sympathised. "But how are you? I know you've been unsettled by the upheaval here, and Lana's case in particular. Are you feeling okay about it all now?"

Bev carefully watched Martha's face, hoping to spot any insincerity. But the young, permanently tired, clinician was hard to read.

"Oh, I'm fine. I've been busy with the others, re-reviewing cases. All my other work has been fine, it's obviously just Lana who had a fault."

Bev raised her eyebrows. "Well, certainly not Lana," she corrected. "Her case, yes, but not her personally."

Anger flared clearly on Martha's face before she stilled it to its customary indecipherable blankness.

"Yes, of course, you two are friends now," she replied. "The review of her results concurred with your decision to clear her record, that must have been a relief for you."

Was there a challenge there? Bev wondered. Or was that just in her exhausted imagination? She knew she must not overreact.

"Indeed, that's been entirely borne out, as expected. We can be glad that we're moving on from it all, and that the process will protect us from any further such situations in future," she worded carefully. "But I'm still worried that you may be harbouring some lingering concerns. No one has or will be blamed for any of this, either internally, or in the coming committee meetings. The focus will be on our process and how our patients are treated afterwards," she stressed.

"Yes, of course," Martha nodded airily. "And I'm fine, honestly. These things happen. I'll just be happy when I'm back working with patients. I need to leave to collect Dana, is that all?"

Bev nodded and said goodnight, rising to pack her own things and head home; yet she was not at all reassured by the conversation. On her way past Peter's door, he called out to her.

"I've just heard from the directorate of health and social care," he sounded appalled. "They're saying that only one problematic case is an aberration, and we should restart the programme immediately, tackle the backlog of referrals. They say we can change the structure of the analysis at our discretion, but halting it is no longer viable."

Bev snapped. "We can't risk taking anyone else

through, if they're going to be at risk of being mistreated as Lana was! I'm not handing any more people that legal agreement knowing that it could potentially be used to force unwarranted compulsory treatment! They'll have to get rid of me first!" she exclaimed, before striding out the door.

Chapter 7 – Tuesday 27th January and Wednesday 28th January

Today, Lind brought in a wash of fresh air and cherry blossom fragrance, and Lana held her friend's welcoming hug a little longer than usual, enjoying seeing them for the first time in too long.

"Let's not leave it this long again," she admitted to Lind, "I've missed you. To what do we owe the unexpected visit?"

Lind had appeared at the door of the garage Lana used as her workshop, wrapped up in woollens and quilting, nose a deep pink in the cold air. Lana shut the door behind her and pulled Lind in front of the old oil-filled radiator which made the working temperature almost bearable.

"Let me just clean up, then we'll head indoors where it's more comfortable," she apologised.

Lind, however, was looking more worried than chilled, and waved off Lana's concerns.

"Don't worry about that," they frowned. "Something

weird happened today at the bank."

Until recently, Lana had worked with Lind at one of the town's local bank branches – in fact she had received her final wages from them just that week, following months of gardening leave as part of her dismissal. They had been wrongly informed that she was mentally unwell and refusing treatment, and when that situation was later rectified, Lana had found herself unwilling to return to the work she had loathed.

Lind continued, "Some woman was in asking questions about you at lunchtime. I got back to my counter, and she was pestering Robert about you, asking if he knew where you worked now."

Lana frowned, unsure who might do such a thing. "I used to have a few regular customers for foreign currency and things, was it one of them?"

"Nope," Lind confirmed. "I didn't recognise her at all. I'd swear she wasn't local; she had an English accent and was dressed straight from the catwalk. Very uptight looking, too," Lind frowned wistfully, "but the most amazing handbag..."

"Well, I'm sure whoever it was will manage without me," Lana laughed. "Unless they want to buy some furniture," she gestured at the pieces lined up in the garage as she switched off the power points and lights. "Let's go get warmed up. Do you have anything organised for tonight? How about I get changed and we can go grab something to eat?"

As they made their plans, and Lana's parents welcomed Lind into their kitchen, Lana gave no more thought to the odd news. Lind could over-dramatise sometimes, and Lana had other things she wanted to discuss with her friend. When she came back downstairs in fresh clothes, however, her parents were not as relaxed.

"Lana, Lind said about this woman who was asking about you, who could it be?" her mum asked.

"Oh, it won't be anything exciting," Lana soothed, "I'm not likely to come into an unexpected inheritance or anything," she laughed. "It was probably just an old customer or something. Sorry for the last-minute dinner plans, Dad," she added.

"No worries," Peter Knight grinned. "I'm not organised with what I'm going to make, anyway. We could get fish and chips or something," he looked at his wife hopefully, as she rolled her eyes fondly.

Later, when the two friends were sitting in warm comfort at a snug corner bar table, Lind giggled. "I wonder if your dad will get his way with his chippy supper?"

Lana grinned, taking her plate from their server, which was enormous and brimming with steak pie and chips and glistening fresh vegetables. "I hope so - if they're having toasties or salad or something I'll feel a bit guilty for eating all of this," she admitted. "Your curry looks wonderful, how is it?"

Lind was just about to try a first mouthful but stopped short and lowered their cutlery back to the plate.

"Lana," Lind hissed, "That's the woman, over there by the big mirror, with the guy with the beard." Lind turned firmly but rather dramatically away from them and looked inquiringly at Lana.

Lana looked over, intrigued. She didn't recognise either person, but she could see what Lind had meant when describing the female: she held herself very rigidly, touching as little furniture as possible, picking at her salad and watching her companion eat with an obvious distaste.

"Definitely not a bank customer," she shrugged, now slightly curious herself. She briefly considered going over and introducing herself, but something held her back, quite possibly just the woman's disdainful sneer. "She obviously doesn't know what I look like, anyway, they're sitting looking right at us," she muttered. "Let's just eat and ignore them."

As Lana finished her meal, however, the two rose from their table, and approached. Interestingly, the man took the lead, turning on a wide smile and folding his coat over his arm before stopping beside Lind.

"Excuse me," he beamed a smile with a polite nod. "But might you be Lana Knight?" He didn't wait for a response, clearly confident of his information. "We were hoping to talk to you about your experiences with Bryant-Cargill factorisation - we've been trying to track you down."

Lana was stunned. Despite the others raising their concerns about the press, she hadn't for a moment thought that her experiences might be interesting enough to warrant any attention. She sat, motionless, aware that Lind was bristling across from her. The woman, however, didn't wait for a reply before interrupting them.

"Are you truly safe to be unmedicated, amongst the public?" she asked, outright. "Do you believe you have any right to be included in the investigative committee, given the concerns about your mental health?"

Lana felt her words like a hard slap and found herself with neither the breath nor an appropriate response with which to retaliate. Lind, however, was already rearing from their seat, protective and angry.

"That's enough! I don't know who you are, but we certainly won't be talking to you about anything! You can back off right now; I'll happily risk being arrested to smack that supercilious face off you!"

For a moment, Lana was frightened Lind would have to follow through on the threat, but the man was already ushering his colleague away from their table and towards the exit.

"People deserve to know what's happened, Ms Knight!" was his parting shot.

John, the owner of the bar, was at their table moments later, concern and alarm in his questions. "Is everything okay, you two? What was that all about?"

Lana was still speechless; Lind took charge. "They're reporters," they spat. "Trying to dig dirt on our Lana just because she's helping the Bryant and Cargill people out." John was shaking his head in confusion, but clearly affronted by the incomers' actions. "Lana's done nothing wrong, she doesn't deserve to be hassled like this when she's out."

Thankfully, John was already nodding. "Absolutely," he agreed. "I hadn't realised who they were; I certainly didn't expect any trouble, or I would have told them they weren't welcome. Will you two be okay?"

Lana knew she should be replying, knew she should be grateful for his concern, but just couldn't quite believe what had happened. She nodded vaguely, looking towards the door before mumbling her thanks. John headed back to the bar, leaving Lind still bristling and Lana weak-limbed.

"The cheek of them!" Lind raged. "Do you want me to call Munro, Lana?"

"No! God, no. He'll have Stuart with him, I don't want him seeing anything like this!" she replied, appalled. "No, we'll just wait a bit then walk back home. We've done nothing wrong; we don't need to worry." Stomach churning, she knew she was as keen to convince herself as much as Lind.

The next day, Lana was helping to look after her nephew, Robbie. He was now fourteen months old, and while he was generally a happy child, he could be as tiring as he was fun. His mum was working reduced hours, and usually had a Wednesday off, but this week she was attending company meetings in Brighton, so Robbie was staying with Lana and her parents. Lana was spending more time indoors than usual, to help.

After coming home from the meal with Lind, Lana had let Munro and Bev know what had happened, using the group chat they had set up. Both had been horrified by the incident, Bev most concerned about how they had found out her details, and Munro most worried about Lana's safety. Now, though, she was determined not to let it ruin her week, focusing on Robbie and the soup she was making for lunch. She was retrieving brightly hued plastic balls from across the floor, and returning them to the pop-up ballpen Robbie adored, when Munro rang.

"They've just been into the surgery, demanding to see a senior partner," Munro opened without pre-amble. "Maria met with them. They know that we're seeing each other, were questioning when that had started and whether the practice was happy that there was no breach of ethics. Maria refused to discuss anything with them, but said they already seem to know a bit about you. They were mostly just looking for confirmation of details. Lana, I don't know how, but she said they knew about specific medications you had been prescribed. This is horrific."

Showering an armful of balls over a giggling Robbie, Lana surprised even herself by laughing abruptly, feeling slightly hysterical. "Well, that didn't take them long. Just as well I have nothing to be ashamed of, really. Well, nothing medical, anyway. They might be able to dig up a story about when I fell out with my first boyfriend, but I doubt that will make exciting headlines," she explained. "How are you? Are you worried? It's not good that they're asking about you as well?"

Munro sighed, and Lana could hear his strong fingers drumming on his desk in the background. "The practice is fine, they know everything. And while they maybe don't wholeheartedly approve because you're an ex-patient, they know we've done nothing wrong. I'm just worried about them coming to the house - I'd hate for any of this to bother Stuart. Maria said they were mostly asking about you, so hopefully they won't think to come here," he muttered. "Oh God, sorry Lana. That came out wrong..."

Lana interrupted him, before he could worry too much. "No, it's fine; I totally understand. The last thing I want is anything upsetting Stuart. You should mention it to

Laurie, make sure she's being careful when she picks him up from school and heads back home. They must be wondering why I'm involved with Bev and the committee; hopefully things will calm down in a few days when they see there's nothing exciting to talk about."

They wrapped up their call, and Lana turned back to the ball pen, where Robbie had once again thrown most of the balls across the floor while she was distracted. Now, he giggled cheekily, and flapped his arms at his sides as if splashing in water; Lana gave in and joined him in his play, grateful for the distraction.

Chapter 8 – Monday 2nd February

Low-level lamps scattered warm light through the room, alleviating the gloom of the deep copper flock wallpaper and rich mahogany of Munro's formal dining room. Lana and Munro sat at the glossy table, his laptop open in front of them, hot drinks steaming gently in delicately painted porcelain mugs perched on coasters. They joined the video call and waited for the others to arrive, glad that Bev had arranged to discuss the latest developments in person.

"I've read so many messages this weekend, I can barely bring myself to look at my phone," Lana grudgingly admitted to Munro. "I never thought so many random strangers would be able to get in touch with me so easily."

Lana had been inundated with unsolicited contact since the news media started reporting on her story, sharing the intimate details of her life for others' salacious enjoyment. She'd had messages of all varieties - some abusing her for spurious reasons, some wanting to support her, some exhorting her to leave Munro, some offering their own sexual advances. She was tired of it all, but more importantly, barely able to find more important messages amongst the clutter; she was seriously considering buying a new number for Munro, her family, and few friends.

They were joined by Bev and Peter from their clinic, followed by Maria from her home office. In the background, a door slammed, and her teenage daughters were heard squabbling vocally; Maria rolled her eyes.

"It'll either be boys, clothes, or hair styling gadgets," she declared. "I've given up trying to referee them for now. If it goes on much longer, I'll send them out to the garden until they cool off."

Lana failed to hide her grin and giggle; she remembered all too well her teenage years with her own sister, and her father's frustrated pleas for peace. Bev was smiling as well, but neither of the men on their call seemed able to enjoy the moment of levity.

"Sorry," Lana apologised. "It's just nice to see someone having an entirely normal time of it," she explained. "Let's get started, I know you're all busy."

Maria took the lead. "The first committee meeting has been set for the 24th, a Tuesday," she reminded everyone. "I've got a documented position from the GP Committee, which Tom has agreed to present. We've also got supplementary material from various other organisations, effectively backing up our position disputing the Bryant Cargill legal agreements when it comes to mental health tribunals. They've documented their recommendations for how the results of the analysis should be managed with the agreement of the patient, rather than enforced. I've sent on copies of everything we have, just shout if you haven't received them."

"Thanks, Maria," acknowledged Peter. "We're ready with our report on the shortcomings of the previous analysis, and we've positioned the changes we'll implement as decisions rather than recommendations, to try and limit any argument. I think we're as ready as we can be. There has been some pressure to restart the programme as-is, until such time as any changes be agreed, but so far, we've managed to push back on that. Long may that continue," he commented. "I think our highest priority at the moment is the handling of this media furore, but we have some news before we get to that." At this he turned to Bev, who had been still at his side throughout.

"I'm afraid I have an apology to make," she explained, taking a breath and staring straight into her camera, the closest to real eye contact she could achieve. "When Lana mentioned that some of the journalists seemed to have knowledge of her clinical details, we instigated a review of our system audit files. All clinical staff theoretically have access to Lana's records; however, no one should have worked on them since I made my updates on Monday 17th November." They all nodded, knowing the reference. "Lana, I'm sorry to say that one of our staff had not only viewed your record on a number of occasions recently, but earlier this month, they printed out your full record. It's not conclusive evidence, but it goes against our data handling procedures, and the staff member had no good excuse when we confronted her. Martha Meziani has been suspended from her duties, the data breach has been reported, and we've reported the situation to the police."

Lana was horrified to see tears in Bev's eyes; in their office, Peter took her hand.

"Lana, I am so very sorry. This is entirely my responsibility. Martha was my hire, data protection is my responsibility, and... Well, we knew she was disgruntled about her diagnosis of you being questioned, but I honestly would never have believed she would do something like this." Bev's voice cracked, disbelief and anger proving too fierce for words.

"Bev, please, no. Don't apologise. You couldn't possibly have known. You trusted her and she's let you down. It's on her, not you," Lana stressed. "Can you tell me exactly what she has passed on? I've never seen my record," she admitted, glancing at Munro, who looked more alarmed than she expected.

"I'll send you a copy," Maria offered. "Or you can come into the surgery to review it with me. In general, it has your basic demographics, plus perhaps older addresses and the like. It documents every visit you've made to a clinician, plus test results, reports from outpatient appointments, notifications of any visits to A&E, that sort of thing."

Munro stepped in. "Lana, they'll have my record of why I referred you to Bryant-Cargill in the first place: your worries, your nightmares, your mood swings."

But Bev then interrupted, even more urgently. "Unfortunately, more was leaked from our end. Our record here also contained a detailed report of everything that was discussed with the team here at the clinic, in both the talking therapies and the analysis, plus what we extrapolated from that, and our eventual diagnosis and treatment plan. When I corrected those, they were additional notes – so I'm afraid everything that Dr Meziani and Dr Fagan diagnosed is still detailed. Admittedly, as historical, inaccurate diagnoses - which my notes clearly refute – but even so. Lana, I'm sorry, but they will have a document of everything you talked through with them."

Lana sat back, thinking through the blur of days she had spent in the clinic, and the wide-ranging discussions they had covered.

"The discussions about my parents and my sister," she immediately realised, with horror. "They could make that sound awful! And we talked over all my old relationships, and all my fears about the moods I get! Oh my God," she gasped, appalled.

"We can raise a court injunction, to stop them releasing any more details to the public. We've already spoken to our solicitors on this end, and we'll work with your solicitor, too, if you'd like. But... yes, they do now know an incredible amount about you," Bev admitted. "We're so sorry."

Lana couldn't stop the tears from coursing down her cheeks, couldn't keep her breath even.

"My family," she forced out. "What will they think? They'll be so hurt!"

Lana bolted out of her chair, grabbing her coat and slamming open Munro's front door in her haste. Young Stuart ran out of the living room, where he had been working on his homework with Laurie, and the tall, compassionate childminder followed him in surprise.

"Lana!" called Munro. "Wait!"

"I've got to get home!" was her only reply, as she sprinted down the drive and off down the street towards her parents' house.

"Dad?" cried Stuart, alarmed and confused. "What's going on, what's wrong with Lana?"

Laurie stood beside him, arm protectively around his shoulders, as Munro turned, the most conflicted he had ever been.

"Daddy?" Stuart repeated, tears starting in his innocent and confused eyes. Eyes tight with anguish, Munro shut the door, and turned back towards his son.

"Hey, don't worry!" he soothed, pulling him into his arms. "Lana just had some news, and she needs to rush home to tell her parents, don't worry. Everything is fine. We'll call her later, like normal. Hey, hey, no tears, she didn't mean to give you a fright. You know how fast she runs: she just didn't expect the door to make so much noise," he added, desperately trying to make Lana's exit seem more everyday. He knelt on the floor and held Stuart, rubbing his back gently before sitting back on his heels and tousling his hair, checking his eyes for fear or upset. He was glad to see his son relax, trusting his father's words.

Once Stuart had calmed, and returned to his reading, Munro headed back to the dining table, fully expecting the call to be ended. But the others were still there, worried and sympathetic expressions on the faces he knew so well. Gratitude welled in him, unexpectedly.

"I'll need to call her," he said, unnecessarily. "But... I guess she'll want to talk to her family first. I hate leaving her to handle it on her own..." he fretted, indecisively.

"Munro," Maria surprised them all by interjecting. "She's strong, she'll be fine. She needs to bring her family up to speed - and whatever was said in the clinic, it sounds like they need time as a family to talk it through. Trust her with this."

Munro slumped into his seat, robbed of any strength in his limbs.

"I was worried enough about what I'd put in my notes," he found himself admitting. "I hadn't even realised that they'd handed over the notes from the clinic, too. Dear God, what a mess."

"I know," Bev agreed. "It's horrific. We can only pray that the people in receipt of those documents have a conscience, or that the court injunction is enough to stop them. All of this, on top of what we were already facing... poor Lana."

Maria looked at her watch. "I'm sorry, but I need to head off shortly. I hate to leave you all, or change the subject, but... Do you need me for anything else?"

"Actually," Peter spoke for the first time since Bev's revelation. "Before we found out about Dr Meziani, there was something I wanted to raise. If that's okay with you all?"

When Munro shrugged, unsure where Peter was going and unable to care about anything other than Lana. Peter continued.

"I don't know if you've seen the outcry online?" The others shook their heads, puzzled. "There's a lot of angry people on the internet, but there are also lots of good groups who use social media to raise awareness of issues. Between both camps, there has been considerable discussion of the moral questions surrounding our work, and how we use the results; to be honest, that's been going on for the last couple of years, off and on. I've been keeping an eye on it. But with everything recently, a couple of groups have realised that civil rights could be being transgressed here in the UK; there's been a lot of discussion about that in the last few days. They're talking about arranging protests, raising public awareness outside of their usual online channels. It may be something we could use, or join, to raise enough public concern about the enforced Compulsory Treatment Order, for example, and make sure that it's knocked on the head. It would be a big step for us, going from quietly influencing back-office committees to becoming involved with pressure groups and protests – but it might help our cause. What do you think?"

The others were silent at first, Munro struggling to focus on the nuances of Peter's suggestion while he was so distracted by worry for Lana, and the others taken aback by this left-field suggestion.

"I think it's got to be worth a try," Bev finally spoke. "At least speak to... someone? Somehow? And see what they think they could achieve in terms of publicity and raising detailed awareness, rather than just noise." She paused, uncertain.

Maria laughed lightly, and added, "When I was a student, we were always protesting something or other. That was before the days of keyboard warriors, of course. We took to city squares with banners, the way the climate change protesters have been. Is that the sort of thing you're suggesting?" she questioned.

"Maybe. I'm not certain," Peter admitted. "I just feel like we should be doing more to ensure we're not forced down a route we're unhappy with."

"Should we hold off and decide after the first committee meeting, see how that goes?" Munro suggested.

"By then, half the committee members will already have decided what they think," Bev posited. "Decisions made over dinners and drinks," she scorned. "I say we strike while the iron is hot, make some fuss," she concluded.

Munro was surprised at her vehemence but knew how much she had feared her work being used inappropriately, and her fierce anger when it had been. Peter was nodding his head in agreement, and even Maria looked invested. He thought of Lana, and how she had been treated, and knew he couldn't advise caution. They agreed that Peter should test the waters.

Chapter 9 – Monday 2nd February and Tuesday 3rd February

The soft, brushed cotton under Lana's cheek was soaked with her scalding tears, but she couldn't seem to stop their flow. Every breath she released seemed laden with grief, the hot hurt too vicious to contain just yet. Around her, the silence of the room was broken only by the ticking of a clock, and the reassuring shush of central heating. She tried to calm herself, focusing on the steady thump of her father's heartbeat where he had gathered her into a hug. Her mother sat on the other side of him, leaning over and gently stroking her hair. She felt like a child, she realised: an ungrateful and spiteful one. She took a deep breath and sat up.

"I'm so sorry," she stammered, yet again.

"Shh, shh," her mum replied, "don't be getting upset again. You're okay, you've not done anything that bad."

Lana could barely believe what she had heard. "Nothing that bad?" she asked. "How can you say that? I talked to that woman about our whole family, and now those awful journalists have it all!"

"Lana, from what you've said, you just answered their questions truthfully – in fact, you spent quite a bit time standing up for us when they made some incorrect assumptions," her mum countered. "Unless you haven't told us everything?" she checked. Lana shook her head miserably. "Well, your sister might be a bit miffed that you told them about some of the arguments you used to have, but other than that there's nothing that bad, is there?" Her parents shared a look here, shrugging.

"Mum, I told them all about you being unwell, and about you and Jen being so close, and me spending more time with Dad, and that I was glad when Jen went off to uni because she annoyed me, but how I didn't want to have to spend more time with you here at home when you felt lonely. And I talked to them about how unfair I used to think it was that I had so few friends when Jen was so popular, and... and I think I even talked to them about how you don't like to go out the house much now!" she blurted.

"Oh Lana," her dad tried to get through to her. "We don't care about any of that, it was all years ago. And there was never any real bad feeling between you girls or anything. When they asked you about that, you told them so, didn't you?" When Lana nodded, he continued. "How we are as a family now, that's what is important. And you're a wonderful daughter, and sister. If all those old things were still worrying you, then, yes, we would have preferred that you talked to us about it, rather than strangers. But these were answers to questions they had asked you: it's okay that you answered them honestly. We aren't going to be hurt by anything we hear you've said – we're angrier that they've broken your confidence this way."

"I think Jen is going to be furious with me," Lana stuttered, realising she was still being childish but somehow unable to control it.

"Jen will be fine: she loves you, and you've done so much for her and Robbie recently. Honestly, it will be okay. What are you and Munro going to do about all this gossip about you, though?"

Lana sat back, the change of tack giving her pause. "Ooft. I don't know. We've just been hoping things would settle down once the committee made its decisions. I still don't get it. I don't understand why they would want to know all those things about me, why they think anyone would be interested."

Peter knew, wisdom gleaned from years of quiet observance. "It's good gossip, Lana, disguised as a public interest story because there's a link to healthcare. But the story they're really selling is that an attractive young woman who thought she had mental health issues brought an award-winning clinic to a standstill. That she has ended up in a potentially influential position with regards to its future. How she ended up in a relationship with the doctor who referred her. They probably don't know yet how they're going to spin it. Will the public feel sorry for you? Were you let down by the system? Or will they attack you because they're jealous that you've come through this successfully? I don't know," he shrugged. "But I do know that however they portray you and Munro, it will be what makes them most money. You need to steel yourself, Lan. But you never have to worry about what we think."

Lana's mum was smiling at her husband warmly, gently nodding her approval. Their affection was solace, and Lana felt the weight shift on her shoulders, but not lift; she hadn't dared tell them the worst of what she had shared with the psychologists, and still feared how her sister would react to what she had said about her.

The next morning, she rose early, hoping to catch Jen before she started her day. As a software developer, she worked from home, taking her son Robbie to a private nursery to spend office hours with other children. For now, her home was Lana's small flat, which Lana had offered to the young family to give them some much-needed space of their own. But Jen's financial separation from her husband had recently completed, and Jen was busy scouting out potential properties of her own. Lana knew that if she didn't catch her early in the day, it could be late evening before they had any time to talk.

As she climbed the steps to the front door, and rang the bell, she realised she was looking forward to moving back into her own space: she missed time to herself, and still felt more at peace here than anywhere else. Jen opened the door promptly, grabbing Lana into an embrace.

"Don't be mad, Mum called me after you went to bed last night. She told me everything; of course, we aren't upset with you. How are you doing?" she asked. "This is awful."

Jen was slightly taller than Lana, with a softer, curvier figure, and wavier hair. She evoked a quietly mature elegance, tending to be more thoughtful and sombre than her younger sister. She had set the benchmark for both beauty and Lana's self-criticism as a teenager, with the result that Lana entirely underestimated her own looks. With less than two years separating them, everything from boys to books had been subjects of contention for a long while.

Lana smiled ruefully as they went into the kitchen and Jen made tea. "They asked me lots of questions, and I stupidly answered them. Just because I talked about it that day, it doesn't mean I still care about those things," she tried to explain.

"I know," Jen readily accepted the explanation. "And so do Mum and Dad. Go on," she grinned. "What's the worst thing you said about me?"

Lana's heart winced. She swore she could feel it physically twist. "I told them about Nathan," she whispered, awkwardly.

Jen's eyes widened slightly in surprise. "What, about thinking I was flirting with him that time?" she asked, perplexed.

"I didn't just think it, you did!" Suddenly, from nowhere, it all came back to her, and she veered from feeling embarrassed to reliving her anger. "I'd been seeing him for months. I honestly thought I was in love with him, and you came swanning home from university and knackered it!" Lana retaliated.

"Oh, bollocks!" Jen exclaimed, before looking sheepishly up the stairs to where Robbie still slept. "I was just being nice; he was the one who tried it on with me! Lana, we went over this a hundred times back then, you know all this. It wasn't my fault he was an unfaithful git."

"You did it with everyone I liked, flirting and showing me up as the lesser sister," Lana snapped. "But that time you went too far, we were really good together."

Jen stood frozen at the fridge door, lost for words and wrestling with her temper, knowing her sister was fragile.

"Okay. So, you're still upset about all that; I thought it

was long forgotten. I'm sorry. I said sorry at the time, that I would never do it again, and I'm pretty sure I haven't."

"No. God, no," Lana interrupted her as her temper cooled as abruptly as it had soared. "Ignore me, honestly, I don't care about that anymore. It's just my stupid brain, it brings ancient things up, and they're just as fresh as ever. I know what he was really like. God, since then I've watched him cheat on every woman he's been with, and he's drunkenly tried it on with me heaven only knows how many times. I know it wasn't your fault, I just lose track of what's real sometimes when I look back on things." She shook her head. "That's part of what made me want to understand myself better in the first place," she admitted. "But now it's just dragged all my petty thoughts out into the open for everyone to see."

They sat down together, tentatively, unsure whether they were okay. Lana could see Jen's mind was at work, and knew she wanted to speak.

"What are you thinking?" she braved.

"Honestly? I worry that you hold all these old hurts and squabbles so tightly, Lana. It can't be good for you. But... Well, the sad truth is that those sorts of stories are nothing. They're not exciting, no one wants to read them. 'Sisters squabbled over daft boy!' is hardly headline news, is it? Are you really worried they'll report on it?" she asked.

Lana pondered for a moment. "That's a good point. I was just terrified, thinking about you all hearing these things and being hurt, and angry with me. But it's not much excitement compared to all the celebrity gossip, is it?" She paused to think. "Realistically, I think they're more likely to use evidence of the Bryant-Cargill diagnosis to try and discredit me, maybe stop me from talking to the committee. But even that, I don't really understand. If they dirty my name, they may be able to bring into doubt whether I should have been cleared? That would make Bev look bad, but why do they care? Ugh. Honestly, I'm just sick of thinking about it, worrying about it all."

Lana covered her face, pushing her fingers along her brows to relieve the tension there. She reached for her mug, and gratefully sipped her tea, glancing at the sister she loved. "Are we okay? I didn't mean to go bonkers on you. I just haven't slept well for days," she admitted.

Jen smiled. "We're fine, of course we are. You need to take care of yourself, though. There's no heading to hide in a cottage in the middle of nowhere this time! You're needed in Edinburgh next month."

"Oh, don't remind me," Lana rued. "And it sounds like there's more happening before then, too!"

She and Munro had messaged late the night before, and he had explained Peter's plan to her. As she related it to Jen, little Robbie finally woke, his sleepy voice calling for his mum from beyond the stairgates. As the two women happily re-focused on the true priorities in their lives, Lana thought of her dad's words the night before. She needed to steel herself, indeed.

Chapter 10 – February

Saturday 7th February

Bev stood forlornly in her kitchen, impatiently waiting for her morning coffee, drip by drip. She had stayed up later than usual last night, watching a film and drinking a bottle of Malbec, nibbling her way through too many salty snacks. As a result, she had slept badly and late, and was now feeling dehydrated and rough. She shifted her gaze from the wind-tossed trees outside her balcony doors, and began silently cataloguing her belongings: sparse furnishings, few ornaments, impersonal paintings. As she turned back towards the kitchen, her fridge contents depressed her further: wine, soft drinks, pickles, chutneys and sauces, a mouldering cheese and a tub of non-butter spread. Her weekend yawned ahead of her like an endless rainy Sunday afternoon, but she felt incapable of deciding how to spend her time without first eating a decent breakfast. She knew the sensible thing would be to shower, dress, and shop for groceries, but instead she threw herself onto her sofa, sipped her coffee, and tried not to think about the emptiness of her life. Free time felt like a burdensome chore after so many years of overwork. If her career was taken from her, she pondered, what would be left?

Five minutes later, she had finished her coffee, pulled a throw over her legs, and was idly considering whether to go back to sleep. Her phone roused her from her reverie, and she smiled as she saw it was Peter calling.

"I'd have thought you were sick of the sight of me?" she half-joked as she answered. She smiled fondly as he rebuked her for it, then brightened visibly as she listened to his news. "Oh, Peter, are you psychic?" she joked. "I have absolutely nothing here; I've been feeling sorry for myself. Your timing is perfect." She rose from her seat and looked down into the carpark of her apartment block, waving at him as he brandished his paper bags. "Come up, I'll make more coffee."

Peter had been to their favourite deli, picking croissants, continental meats and cheeses, and sweet, sticky pastries. He might never know how much she appreciated it.

"I figured you might not want to tackle a supermarket this morning," he posited, showing once again the keen eye and sympathy she often forgot he had. "It's been some week; I figured you deserved a little looking after." He scrutinised her momentarily. "You look worse than I usually do on a weekend morning. You're always scolding me about getting too old to be up late in clubs and the like – it's not like you to be worse for wear."

The breath Bev released was half sigh, half laugh. "I wish I had been to some wild night out last night, but it was just me and Casino Royale." Bond films were her favourite distraction. "But, yeah, it's my own fault I'm hungover and didn't sleep well. It seemed like a good idea at the time," she grinned ruefully. "As it always does! I'm feeling better now, though, thanks."

"I heard back from the guy who seems to head up that civil rights action group," Peter pivoted. Bev sat forward with interest. "He wants to talk to us, he's keen to get us involved in a march he's organising here in Edinburgh. They're incensed by what they've heard. I said we could fill him in on our concerns, see what we think about what they have planned. Did I do the right thing?"

Bev was already nodding fiercely. "Hell, yes. The only thing we had to lose was Lana's privacy, and that horse has bolted thanks to bloody Martha." Peter wondered briefly if Bev would ever again say her ex-employee's name without swearing. "We've nothing to hide, nothing to lose. We need people to realise how important the decisions will be when the committee convenes, get them to start pressurising their MPs, create a groundswell," she enthused, much more like her usual self. "This is perfect."

Monday 9th February

Lana and Munro exited the video call and sat back on the sofa. Stuart was already in bed upstairs, and they were glad: the call had been exciting, but what they were planning wasn't something he could attend. He would be peeved if he heard about it.

Bev and Peter had arranged for them to join a march on Saturday. Not only that, but the organisers wanted them to speak at the rally which would kick off the protest, highlighting the main concerns they had about how their analysis results had been taken as gospel by the wider NHS and used to circumvent the fair handling of mental health patients. Maria had surprised them all by being the most enthusiastic: her passion for protecting her patients was fierce. Lana and Munro had agreed that Lana would attend, but Munro would have to stay home with Stuart, as Laurie had a family wedding. He wasn't at all comfortable with it.

"I don't like this," he summarised, not surprising Lana at all. "You'll be exposing yourself to a huge crowd. The media won't overlook you if you take centre stage – literally – at such a large event. I can't believe I can't even be there with you," he fretted.

"Don't worry so much." Lana understood his concern, but thought it was disproportionate. "Bev, Peter and Maria will all be there with me. And Peter says the group leading this are really quite savvy and organised, you heard how impressed he was." Munro still looked unconvinced. "And to be honest, I'm already in the media's line of fire, and it will only get worse after the committee convenes and reports to the parliament. I might as well do this on my own terms - do some good at the same time. You know we can't let anyone else be treated the way I was," she culminated forcefully.

Munro sighed, stood and gathered their mugs from the table. "Would you like another?" he asked.

But Lana could tell he was still unhappy. "Not yet; leave those for now. Please, tell me what it is that has you so worried. What's the worst that could happen?"

Munro settled back into the sofa, taking her hand. He thought for some time, then spoke just as Lana thought she would need to prompt him once more.

"I'm frightened of you getting hurt. Both physically –

sometimes these protests turn nasty – and by what will be said about you during this whole endeavour," he admitted. "I'm frightened that they'll make an even bigger deal of our relationship, make it seem wrong... or seedy. I'll look like I took advantage of you when you were low," he confessed, "or they could make you look weak, unstable, needy." He saw Lana bristle, and assumed she was about to tell him he was over-worrying. "I'm serious, Lana. Doctors really aren't meant to date patients; they could make a big deal of this."

But Lana wasn't concerned he was over-worrying at all; she was startled at how he seemed to perceive them both.

"What on earth makes you say that?" she asked, uncertain if she was being too prickly. "Why would they think our relationship was seedy? Or that I'm needy? What does that have to do with you being a doctor?"

Munro fought down the panic he always felt when he might have upset Lana. "I just worry what those types of media people might think of it. I mean, they exaggerate for effect, so they might say those sorts of mad, extreme things. Obviously, no one sensible would say that," he blustered, hoping he hadn't gone too far.

"Oh, for God's sake, I'm not going to bite you," Lana snapped. "You don't need to look so frightened of me. I just wanted to know why you would say that. You make me feel like an ogre when you act like this!"

Munro was trapped between two impossible choices. Say nothing and continue looking wary of her or continue his point and put his foot in it again. The full truth - how frightened he was of upsetting her, losing her - seemed impossible to reveal at this juncture. Thankfully, she saw his dilemma, her anger cooled, and she apologised quickly.

"Sorry, I didn't mean to snap at you. No wonder you're acting like I'm about to fly off the handle! I've been so out of sorts, recently," she lamented.

"No, it was my fault," Munro disagreed. "You're fine, I'm the one worrying about mad nonsense. Can we put this behind us?" As Lana nodded, he returned to the coming protest. "Are you sure you'll be fine on Saturday?" he checked.

"Yes," was the firm reply. "Honestly, Munro, I'll be there with the others and doing something worthwhile. I care about this. You're acting like I'm attempting the pinnacle of Sgurr Dearg in flipflops," she joked, grouchily. This was one of her dad's favourite expressions for an impossible or dangerous task, and she enjoyed seeing the momentary confusion on Munro's usually unflappable features, before he realised her gist. She watched him graciously acquiesce despite his worries, loving him for it.

Chapter 11 – Thursday 12th February

"No Munro again!" exclaimed Ailsa. "I know you haven't made him up entirely, but I'm beginning to believe he actually lives in Greenland, rather than Broughty Ferry," she griped.

Lana grinned at Ailsa's annoyance: she had only met Munro once, very briefly, and it continued to rankle her that some of the others had been given more opportunities to get to know the new man in Lana's life.

"Sorry, Ails," she accepted, "he's got lots of running around to do with Stuart, and work to catch up on. He's not avoiding you... well, not all of you," she added, kicking Sanj's feet off her hand-upholstered footstool. "Mucky trainers off before you do that," she advised, mock-sternly. "It's a Lana Knight, you know," she laughed.

It was Jen's turn to host movie night, and Lana had been looking forward to it all week: despite having so much on her plate, there was no way she was missing her friends again. It was always odd for her to be in her own flat, using her own furniture, eating from her own crockery... as a guest. But she loved the camaraderie of this group and loved these evenings of jamming themselves into sofas and chairs, lounging around and sharing snacks. It made her feel like a teenager again.

Colin and Ailsa settled into one end of the oversized sofa, and as they snuggled in, they shared a quick kiss, a look of happy affection in both their eyes. Lana felt a deep satisfaction on seeing their contentment, and privately thought they would be the first of their friends to get married or have children. It seemed no time at all since she and Colin had shared a desk on their first day of secondary school, he a tiny, skinny boy with huge glasses and a wilful crown in his hair, while she was nervy and sensitive about her new uniform, and the braces in her teeth.

Tonight's entertainment was the latest in a long series of comic book adaptations, with the world's favourite actor in the lead role. Jen was dishing out popcorn, crisps and dips, and finger food, when Lind arrived, late as always, but cheerful enough to be immediately forgiven.

"What do you think?" they demanded, giving a twirl as they removed their long wool coat. Movie night was traditionally about comfort over style, something Lind rarely chose, but the stunning burgundy velour co-ordinates with sequinned lilies across the collarbones was a fantastic departure into loungewear. Lana freely admitted she was jealous, declaring "first dibs" on the outfit when Lind inevitably grew bored of it. Lind squeezed into the spot between Sanj and Ailsa, and the evening could start.

The film was near-constant action, so they paused often to refill drinks, visit the bathroom, and fetch more food. Over the evening, Lana noticed that Lind and Sanj always seemed to end up sitting beside each other, and idly wondered if Lind's interest in Sanj had been rekindled since he had split up with his girlfriend, Esme. She resolved to keep an eye on them, and as she glanced away, she caught Jen's eye and a knowing twinkle in it. By the end of the film, Lind had rested their head on Sanj's shoulder, and the pair looked remarkably comfortable in each other's space. Lana resolved to walk Lind home, to be nosey.

They lingered after the film, comparing opinions and laughing again at the most outrageous scenes. Lana told the others about her plans for the march in two days' time, feeling slightly disappointed when they all approved, but only Lind committed to joining her.

"Oh, Lana, I would love to come," Ailsa professed. "But I'm not good with large crowds, and I hate hanging around."

The others all had their excuses, too, ranging from the practical – a toddler - to the less believable – helping an uncle move a piano. Lana laughed it off, though, knowing her friends weren't political animals, and content with the company she would already have.

As they went their separate ways at the junction along from the flat, Lana took Lind's arm, and offered to share the walk home. They said their goodbyes to the others and headed away from the beach, past houses and Lana's favourite church, with its renowned stained-glass windows, and renovated steeple. The gardens were always maintained beautifully by the congregation, but at this time of year it was a leaf-strewn and wormcast-riddled mess. A banner on the church hall proclaimed Saturday evening's St Valentines cheese and wine night, and Lana felt a clench of worry.

"Oh no, with everything else that's going on, I didn't think about Valentines," she confessed. "I hope Munro didn't have plans."

"I imagine he did," Lind retorted. "Or certainly something that didn't involve you being in Edinburgh, anyway. What time will we get home, will you have time for a nice dinner together?"

"I hope so," Lana offered uncertainly. "I wonder if Mum and Dad would mind me commandeering the kitchen," she mused. "Do you have any plans?" she asked.

Lind shrugged non-committally and perhaps overly casually. "Nah, I've been taking a break from dating, you know? I'm not making a big deal about it, it'll just be me and some fizz and some dark chocolate, I expect."

"I wondered if there might be someone you had your eye on," Lana probed, mimicking Lind's overly casual demeanour.

"I know you're fishing!" was her sharp-tongued reward, and the two laughed at their own posturing. Lind sobered. "Honestly, I'm not sure what to think. I've no idea whether he likes me, or if he would even consider someone non-binary. I've never seen any prejudice, or judgement, from him; but there's also very few signals. But we get on so well, we're so comfortable together, he touches me and I'm sure it's affection. Oh, I don't know..." they finally tapered off, exhibiting more frustration than Lana had expected.

"It is Sanj we're talking about, isn't it?" Lana gently pried. When Lind nodded, uncertainly and vulnerably, she felt a rush of compassion for her best friend. "I don't know either," she admitted. "He's only ever dated girls; he hasn't ever mentioned anyone else... Oh, you know what I mean. Sorry, I don't know how to word it, and I should."

Lind shook their head. "Don't worry, not many people would; you're doing pretty well. He hasn't ever admitted fancying a glamorous non-binary pansexual, then," they laughed, proving less easily offended than most would believe.

Lana sadly nodded in agreement. "But that means nothing. Maybe he's unsure of what to say or do, too. Maybe he's just not made it clear yet: Sanj has always been cautious with his feelings, Lind." Lana blushed, knowing that the one time he had been bolder had been with her, and that his timing had been appalling; they had agreed to remain friends. "I honestly don't know for sure. If you want, I could try to talk to him, discreetly?" she offered.

But Lind visibly recoiled from that offer. "Oh God, no, that could ruin everything. I'd rather stay friends than do that."

Lana was initially surprised, but on reflection she realised that the statement told her everything she needed to know regarding how Lind felt about Sanj. She was both touched, and a little worried, for her friend.

After she had seen Lind to their door, Lana briefly turned back towards the water, then passed the primary and secondary schools before heading back towards her parents' house. She took the chance to call Munro while she was away from any residential houses, and unlikely to disturb anyone having an early night.

"Everyone missed you," she opened. "Ailsa is beginning to think you're avoiding her!"

Munro could occasionally take things too seriously, but he was beginning to learn when Lana was teasing him; he laughed this off.

"So, I had forgotten that Saturday was Valentines," Lana continued, "too long being single," she laughed. "I'll be back in the evening, would you like to go out someplace, or maybe I could cook?" She paused to listen. "Oh, of course! I'd forgotten that Laurie was away! Well, why don't we have a nice dinner at yours, then? I'll bring the makings, and we can cook together. We keep promising to do that," she reminded him.

Plans made, they said their goodbyes, and Lana crept quietly into her family home, trying to make as little noise on the stairs as she could. She felt like a teenager again. The sooner Jen found a house, the better, she thought.

Chapter 12 – Friday 13th February

Lana and Lind stopped short in the doorway, assaulted by noise, and shared a look.

"They said to meet them in some sort of back room, right?" Lind checked.

"If we can get to it," Lana exaggerated, scanning the crowded bar for a route through the masses. "Let's try this way," she added, taking Lind's hand. "Maria is coming through tomorrow morning, but Bev and Peter should both be here by now, so we'll know the right table."

This was their first proper meeting with the protest organisers, to finalise the plans for the next morning. Lana felt irrationally nervous and was glad Lind had come with her. They had stashed their luggage in their hotel room before dashing across town in order to arrive only a little late.

As they wound through the after-work revellers, Lana spotted the entrance to what she hoped was the back room, and led Lind down a short, narrow, draughty corridor and around a corner. The sudden sense of space in this quieter area was disconcerting after manoeuvring past so many bodies; Lana felt almost as if she was intruding on a private function. They paused momentarily in the doorframe, unconsciously mimicking their entrance from outside, even glancing at each other in the same fashion. Bev and Peter both grinned cheerfully, waving them in towards the large table they had booked.

"Lana!" Bev called in welcome. "In you come, glad you could make it!"

There were plenty of seats, so Lana chose one of two nearest the door, glad there was room for Lind beside her. She looked across the table as she removed her scarf and coat; Bev continued to make introductions.

"This is Chris and Martha," she opened, gesturing to the new faces seated across from her and Peter. "Together, they head up the group who have organised everything."

Sitting opposite Bev was a younger man: perhaps mid-twenties, Lana estimated. He had shoulder-length dark-blonde hair and a scruff of light beard hid his jawline. He was dressed in tired jeans and an ancient REM t-shirt, and when he briefly smiled his welcome, Lana was taken aback by gleaming and perfectly straight teeth, belying his otherwise untidy appearance. His eyes were a deep brown, almost black, and she decided he might be a hard character to read. In contrast, Martha seemed warmer and more welcoming. Older than the others, she had hip-length, highlighted, wavy hair, and minimal makeup other than a deep bronze lipstick. Her look was also casual, although incredibly feminine, with a warm, longline, wool cardigan over a floaty, floral dress better suited to idyllic summer days. Her face was friendly in a maternal way, and she seemed genuinely overjoyed to meet them, setting Lana's nerves at ease a little. Lana felt over-dressed: whenever she was out with the more glamourous Lind, she put in a little more effort, but the others were all very casual. She put it out of her mind, perturbed at her unexpected insecurities.

"Hi!" Lana returned their greetings. "This is my friend Lind, come to join us. Sorry we're late - our train arrived on time, but it just took longer to walk to the hotel than we expected," she explained apologetically.

Lind waved demurely as Lana spoke. "Nice to meet you all," they added, uncharacteristically tentative.

"We've already got some drinks," Peter took over. "What would you both like?"

As he headed to the bar, the others settled back into their seats and chitchatted about their respective journeys into town. Peter and Martha had travelled up from Manchester the day before and, although they were both familiar with Scotland's capital, they had spent the day reconnoitring the march route and checking for last-minute roadworks or issues.

"It's not a massively long distance," Martha explained, "But you'll be amazed how long it takes to get people organised and walk a short way as a group."

"I've never been on a march or anything," Lana confessed. "I have no idea what to expect."

As Peter returned with drinks, Martha detailed the plan for the next day, and advised the others on what to expect.

"Dress warmly, there will be a lot of hanging around. The spirit tends to be quite jovial, almost festival-like, unless there is anyone blocking us or troublemaking. But we don't expect anything like that - it'll be peaceful, I'm sure," she continued. "We're expecting perhaps up to a couple of thousand attendees," she surprised Lana. "As people have learned more about what's happening here, resistance has really risen."

Once they had agreed their plan of action, they continued to get to know each other, their joint purpose lending a comradeship Lana hadn't expected. Chris and Martha's anecdotes of other protests seemed slightly surreal to Lana, and she realised with a jolt that she would have her own story to tell after tomorrow.

Lind had been uncharacteristically quiet throughout, though Lana suspected they were simply not as caught up in the groups endeavours as she was. She remained hugely grateful for the company, though: Lind was the most normal thing here for Lana, which would have made her friend smile. When they rose to fetch some more drinks, she was surprised to see Chris slide over into their vacated seat, bringing the dregs of his pint with him.

"So, you're the girl who survived the threat of incarceration, eh?" he asked, quietly, his dark eyes penetrating.

Lana nodded, uncertain whether she was being mocked. "Well, yes," she agreed. "But only because Munro – my partner – knows Bev and Peter from their student days. Anyone else would have been helpless against the Central Care team when they wanted to commit me, force me to take the medications they insisted were necessary. It's so important we make sure that can never happen to anyone else," she stressed, hoping she wasn't sounding too serious. "That's why I'm here."

Chris had a knowing, lightly amused, gleam in his eye. "Yes, we know the story. You'll be surprised how many people do: almost everyone there tomorrow will," he clarified. "So where is your Munro tonight?" he asked. "Why is your friend here instead, when they're clearly not interested?"

Lana felt herself tense at his disparaging tone. "Lind cares very much about this," she corrected him. "And so does Munro. He can't come through this weekend, though, he has his son to look after." Realising she was justifying his absence to a stranger, she felt flustered, and was relieved to see Lind return with the last of the drinks.

With a pointedly raised eyebrow and suggestive smirk, Lind settled into the seat Chris has abandoned, and turned to Martha, joining her discussion with Bev and Peter. Lana heard Lind ask how the civil rights group was funded, holding back a smile; Lind could be incisive at times.

The evening passed pleasantly, as they all got to know each other a little, and shared their concerns. Despite differences in politics and preferred causes, they all brought a drive to defend the rights of others, which Lana found heart-warming. She learned that Martha had been protesting since she had been a student council leader, bringing more than twenty-five years of experience to the table. Chris, a self-titled social media influencer, brought a passion for raising awareness of the issues he championed, and despite being younger and from a more privileged background than Martha, he shared her outrage at the unfairness they saw in society. Between them, they balanced responsibility for an organisation that was involved in more campaigns than she had expected. Their proficiency was reassuring.

As they left the bar, and said their farewells, Lind took

Lana's arm and turned in the direction of their hotel.

"That Chris fancies you," they stated, bluntly.

Lana was surprised at both the statement and their matter-of-fact tone. "No," she automatically refuted, before she had really thought it through. "It didn't seem that way to me," she added, a little less certainly.

Lind raised their brows in question. "Really? He watched you like a hawk all evening. He was snarky about Munro, at least twice that I overheard. He made a very big deal of how wonderful you are for dealing with everything, wanting to fix the bigger issues."

Lana bristled. "Well, quite a few people have said that. It would be easier to be selfish about it, just be glad that I'm safe now, and put it behind me. I mean, I'm not looking to be lauded for it or anything, but I think it's okay for him to say those things," she ended, suddenly realising she was being too sensitive. "Sorry, I didn't mean to snap," she added.

Lind squeezed her arm where they held it. "I'm not saying that he isn't right to be impressed with you: I'm saying that he went on a bit too much about it and was eyeing you up all night. I don't know, Lana, but he just didn't seem quite right to me. One minute, too cool to talk; the next, too flattering by far. Separating you off from the rest of us, talking quietly so it was just you who could hear your conversations. Red flags, Lan," they pointed out, not flinching from their opinion.

But Lana hadn't seen any of that. "No, he was just a bit more reserved than Martha, that was all," she found herself defending him. "Anyway, I doubt we'll see much of him tomorrow, and then it's all over. There's nothing to worry about," she added firmly, shivering in the cold night air and picking up the pace.

Chapter 13 – Saturday 14th February

The next morning, Lind and Lana arrived where they had arranged to congregate, stunned at the number of attendees already present. They worked their way through the shifting crowds, heading towards the steps of a statue which Chris had advised they would use as a makeshift podium. Lana's nerves were taut, knowing that most of the speaking would be done by others, but still worrying that she would somehow mess things up. As they approached, she saw that everyone else was already there: Peter looking tired and a little bamboozled, while Maria and Bev looked determined and eager. Peter waved.

"Hi! I can't believe how many people are here!" he called. "Isn't this amazing?"

Lana agreed. There was something of a holiday spirit about the crowd, a light-heartedness more in line with a concert or an appearance by someone famous. People held banners and flags, ready to move at any time. Most clutched hot drinks, and carried backpacks, as she did. She wondered if they all contained extra layers of clothing, snacks and drinks, like hers: she had no idea how long this would all take.

"Lana, Bev," Martha interrupted her reverie. "Are you both ready? It's nearly time," she advised.

They had agreed that Chris would open the day, reviewing the basics of the march and piquing the crowd's interest. He would then hand over to Bev, and then finally Lana, before he said his final words and co-ordinated the march's direction via helpers scattered through the crowds. Lana felt a surge of excitement despite her wariness, and stood off to one side, marvelling at the effortless way Chris caught and held everyone's attention. She noticed he used the phrase self-determination over and over, realising that it had been used increasingly in the emails and messages they had shared. Chris and Martha felt that this was the core of their fight – everyone's right to determine their own future, including medical care. For Lana, perhaps for everyone here, the expression had moved from being unfamiliar buzzwords, to summarising a basic human right.

As Bev took over, explaining her horror at her legal agreements being used to enforce care, Lana sensed the crowd becoming more agitated, less festive. There was true anger here, and a shared focus on protecting everyone in future. Despite her familiarity with it all, Lana was still impressed as Bev's determination influenced the crowd, the mood turning from jovial to forceful during her short speech. Bev moved off to one side, and Chris stepped back up.

"And now, I'd like you all to meet someone, who I think is going to be important. Someone who has been unjustly pursued by both the NHS, and their now-lackeys, Police Scotland. Someone who, if she had not fought, would have been committed into care for no good reason! Who would have been forced to take not just unnecessary anti-psychotics and anti-depressants - but dosed with unagreed contraceptives! This woman started the fight against this alone, frightened but determined! Will we let her stand alone any longer?" he demanded.

As the crowd bellowed their commitment to Lana's cause, she could barely stop herself from shaking. The emotional rush, the heady encouragement from the massed supporters, the nervous energy while waiting for her turn to speak, had all peaked. She stepped up beside Chris and raised her hand high in the air.

"Thank you!" she cried, hoping her voice carried well enough. "Thank you all for giving your time today to raise awareness of this issue. No one should be incarcerated and medicated without having a fair tribunal! No one should be forced to take medications they can't stop or change when they need to! No one should lose their job because they won't give up control of their own body! Self-determination is a right!"

The crowd cheered massively after each statement, living every word with her. Lana calmed her tone a little.

"We march today, to say "No!" We will not give up our rights to basic freedoms which should be protected by law. Our bodies and minds are our own! We will be heard!"

The crowd roared, and Lana stepped aside, abandoning any thought of saying more; she couldn't imagine the crowd becoming more animated than it already was. She looked to Chris in her confusion, and he grabbed her and Bev's hands and raised them together.

"We march to Holyrood!" he cried. "The government will hear our voices!"

They headed off, Chris leading Lana and Bev, followed by Peter, Maria and Lind. Martha and others corralled the first crowds, and they took their time forming the lines of their march. Lana couldn't quite believe the time it took to organise everyone and get them heading in the right direction at a reasonable pace.

Over the course of the next two hours, she was greeted and welcomed by many of the crowd, Chris by her side. Whenever she glanced around, however, she was comforted by familiar faces: Maria and Bev thoroughly enjoying themselves, chanting and grinning with the column of people, Peter and Lind chatting amiably, laughing at jokes no one else could hear in the tumult. Chris took her arm, reminding her of Lind and what she had said the night before.

"So, what are you doing with yourself now that you aren't working at the job you lost?" he asked.

Lana explained her new business venture, and the joy she found in reworking old furniture. Chris listened attentively as she let her enthusiasm show, smiling when she shook her head and apologised for rambling on.

"God, no, I love it when people are doing something they're passionate about. Your face lights up when you talk about your work, Lana. I'll have to see it some time. What does your Munro make of it all?" he quizzed her.

"Oh, he's really happy for me, he's been so supportive from the start," she explained. "He knew how unhappy I was at the bank and sees how much less..." she struggled for the right words, "constrained I am now. Now I just need to get back to earning some reliable money from it all," she laughed.

"Maybe that won't suit Munro, though," Chris replied. Lana was taken aback, and confused, wrinkling her forehead in response.

"If you're independent again, he loses out," Chris explained. "So far in your relationship he's been an older, wealthier, controlling partner. He was your doctor; his position of authority was set before you ever started seeing each other. That's why clinicians aren't meant to see patients: because even afterwards, the clinician is still an authority figure to the patient. The patient doesn't have entirely free will - not the best grounding for a couple," he continued, oblivious to Lana's growing distress. "He might not be aware of it, but that will be working to his advantage. Anything you do to become more independent of him works against him."

Lana finally found the words to differ. "No, that's not the way it is at all. And he certainly doesn't have any advantage. Trust me, we're fine – we're equals," she managed. "But what do you mean, he's an authority figure?"

Chris was still holding her arm, smiling apologetically at her now. "Sorry, I'm always too forward about things. It's just, I thought it was quite well-known: clinicians, solicitors, the police, people like that, they're natural authority figures. You go to them with problems, they have the solutions. So, we're programmed to defer to them, and to appreciate them more than other people. We let them tell us what to do, often without ever thinking about it. If you get into a relationship with one, you're automatically going to let them take the lead with it. Perhaps you haven't had that, though. You could be the exception to the rule."

Lana's first instinct was to dismiss Chris' concern, but something in what he said sowed a seed of doubt. She had been attracted to Munro at such a difficult time, he had helped her so much, had been the one person she could talk to. Had that influenced her? Was their relationship based on that? She thought of his quiet concern for her this weekend, and supportive acceptance of her decision to speak today; she shook her head firmly.

"No, Munro and I aren't like that," she replied firmly, finally managing to extricate her arm from his grip. "I'm going to check in with Lind, see how they're all doing," she tipped her head towards her friends. "Catch you later." She worked her way through the throng and found Lind and Peter.

"What's up?" Lind asked immediately, always perceptive.

"Nothing," Lana brushed off the question. "How are you all getting on? We must be nearly there by now. What do we do when we get to the parliament buildings?" she asked.

Peter answered. "The plan is to deliver our petition; Martha is in charge of that. They won't let many of us right up to the doors, so when we arrive, we'll wait a bit then disperse. The local pubs will be mobbed afterwards," he mused. "Maybe we should have booked somewhere to eat, I'm starving."

Lind looked deliberately at Lana. "We need to be back in Dundee for six at the latest," she replied. "But we could grab something light? It's been ages since breakfast, and Lana's chocolate stash has run out," they laughed.

As the others picked Peter's memory of bars and restaurants nearby, and Maria searched her phone maps for ideas, Lana pondered the day. She had expected to feel more of a sense of achievement; disbanding and going to eat seemed too mundane a way to wrap up their day. Moreover, she felt dispirited after such an exciting morning: such an immediate return to her normal life seemed jarring to her.

As they arrived at the parliament buildings, Lana eyeballed the large police presence, knowing she shouldn't be surprised but still feeling they were somehow incongruous. As Martha and Chris went into the entrance to deliver the printed petition, the crowd re-gathered, calmer and less vocal than at the start of the march. She smiled as she heard most people's conversations also turn to food, drinks and toilet facilities. Practicalities always dominated, she realised. They milled around for perhaps another half hour, waving their banners and placards at some photographers and a news film crew, before the crowd gradually became noticeably less dense.

"Come on," Peter announced, as Bev joined them. "Let's go eat."

Maria sighed with relief. "Thank goodness," she admitted. "I'd forgotten how long these things go on for. I'm ravenous, and my feet are aching. You young ones have it lucky," she joked.

They headed back towards the Canongate, passing the closest venues before heading into an old, atmospheric pub building. Peter had called them as they hung around, and they had set aside a table for five. They ordered drinks and late lunches, enjoying the warmth and surroundings.

"Maybe we should have invited Martha and Chris?" Bev asked, a little late.

"They were dealing with the last of the crowds," Peter advised. "As organisers, they prefer to stay until everyone is fully dispersed. They're so efficient – much more so than I would have been," he confessed. "They even have volunteers who wait with them and tidy up any excess litter and the like."

Maria was impressed at this last news. "That's certainly better than we used to be back in the day," she mused. "I was mortified after one anti-apartheid event I attended. We walked back the same way later that night, and the mess was unbelievable," she admitted.

"That'll keep them busy," Lind agreed. "Hopefully they'll be pleased with how it all went. Certainly, there were enough attendees to make the politicians realise they need to do the right thing." Lind was watching Lana carefully. "Lana, are you okay? You're very quiet?"

Lana was still feeling displaced, deflated. "I guess I'm just a bit tired. Being back in the warm, having lunch – I feel much better, but a little sad it's all over," she confessed. "I'm not sure I liked being the centre of attention, but it was so empowering to be part of such a big movement," she shrugged dispiritedly.

Maria laughed, then explained, "I think everyone involved always feels like that – it's a real let-down after all the excitement. We used to stay out in the pubs and drink too much, every time," she added. "Pity we've got to get the train home," she raised her mostly empty glass mock-ruefully.

"Yes, home," Lana replied, quietly. "Munro and I are cooking together tonight; he was choosing the menu. That all seems like another world just now." Realising the others were looking at her with concern, she laughed off her wistfulness. "I think all the attention has gone to my head!"

Bev grinned mischievously. "If I know Munro, he'll be showering you with attention tonight, too. I'm surprised your phone hasn't been ringing all day."

Lana smiled, knowing she was right, and resolved to put on an enthusiastic facade until she felt the emotion for real.

Chapter 14 – Monday 16th February

Bev hated visiting this building. It was a grim concrete mass, dotted with small windows, and split into offices for various NHS departments and their visitors. Car parking was minimal, so she tended to stop at the nearby retail park and make the short walk over. But despite the bright, dry weather, she had struggled today. She had been short on time and was now equally short on breath as she juggled her bags and coat through security. Passing along corridors, she saw faces she knew and liked – but today, she wouldn't have stopped to speak even if she was running early; she was filled with a gnawing tension which stemmed from her reluctance to heed the demands of her employers. As she climbed the last few stairs towards the austere meeting room, she took a few deep breaths, and hoped she wouldn't appear as flustered as she felt.

She had spent the day before working through multiple strategies for this discussion, yet she still felt unprepared. The invite had been too vague – while she suspected what would be discussed, she was wary of a last-minute twist in the tale. So, instead of being able to relax after Saturday's protest, she had spent her Sunday tense and disgruntled. Now, she felt tired, irritable, edgy, and fatalistic. She hoped she was merely being cynical, understanding entirely what Lana meant when she said that being self-aware was a pain. The thought of her new friend briefly lifted her spirits before she straightened her shoulders and entered the fray.

"Dr Cargill, good to see you, please take a seat. A shame Dr Bryant can't make it," a deep voice, tinged with sarcasm, welcomed her. This was her boss's boss, a man she met with rarely. He had used her first name on previous occasions, so now Bev instinctively steeled herself for the anticipated criticism. The woman who was officially Bev and Peter's employer sat off to one side, her carefully blanked expression and rigid shoulders belying the rest of her relaxed posture. She met Bev's gaze briefly but gave nothing away. Bev settled into the chair nearest the door, steeling herself.

By the end of the meeting, she was no more inclined to stop and chat to passing colleagues. In truth, it was all she could do to moderate her pace and refrain from snarling at the few people who crossed her path. It had been a long time since she had been reprimanded in the way she had just experienced, and her temper raged, desperate for an outlet. She stormed through the exit and into the fresh air, suddenly glad she didn't have the convenience of her car nearby; she couldn't have driven safely in this mood. She lengthened her stride, cleansed her lungs with deep breaths, and headed away from the offices and the censure she had suffered.

How dare they? How dare they imply she was unprofessional. Working all the hours she did, week in and week out, wasn't enough for them - they thought they could criticise her choices in her own time as well? The protest had been public knowledge for weeks; indeed, she had been the one to let them know about it, with full disclosure. If they'd had a problem with it, they should have said beforehand, not now. To wait until afterwards, then imply her attendance showed a conflict of interest - that was deeply unfair.

But, worse, to question whether she was being entirely honest about her programme, to demand that she restart seeing patients immediately – what were they thinking? Slide after slide of her carefully prepared material had been ignored, leaving her arguments and proposals in the dust. A threat to halt her salary until the programme was back up and running had been the final blow she could endure; she had left before burning bridges she had carefully constructed during years of effort. She could see the shopping centre now, and on impulse she headed toward the nearest doors, rather than her car. She needed coffee – and cake.

Thankful that the small seating area was quiet, Bev leaned back and savoured her first mouthful of chocolate fudge cake, resisting the urge to hurry, to gorge herself. Instead, she paced herself, enjoying the moist sponge and decadent icing, washed down with sips of excellent black coffee. She knew that sugar and caffeine were far from ideal for tension, but contrarily revelled in the small rebellion of indulging herself in work hours. Soon enough, she would have to return to the clinic, and the discipline her work demanded. She took her time, watching families with young children as they noisily navigated the shops and stalls, gradually setting aside the affront she felt, and beginning to enjoy the impromptu break.

As she finished her return journey, and drove back into the clinic carpark, she thought again of the restraints her work placed on her. There were so few people who really knew her: knew her sense of humour, her politics, her moral compass. Her work limited how freely she could talk to her colleagues and her patients, while leaving her little time to socialise with anyone else. Spending more time with Munro and Lana recently had opened a small window into the more open lives most other people lived – free with their opinions, candid with their thoughts. She hadn't realised how much she had missed close friendships; Peter had been her only confidante for some years. Bev smiled, seeing the subject of her ruminations enter the carpark on foot.

"How was it?" she called, as she locked her car doors.

"Long! And awkward," he replied. "They're both keen for her to take some work she's been offered in Ottawa, so most of the chat was about her career and plans. But the food was good, and Sophie came away happy; that's what counts."

Peter had been meeting Sophie's parents for the first time, a lunch date while they were visiting from London. When he and Bev were both invited to attend the management meeting, he had offered to cancel, but Bev had insisted he stick to his plans and had made believable excuses on his behalf. Now, she was especially glad that one of them had avoided the unpleasantness. She held off on her news until they were both in the quiet of her office, knowing that their team would quickly disseminate any rumour of dissent in the chain of command. Peter sat forward as she finished relating the discussions.

"Well, we knew this might happen. Has it changed how you feel at all?" Bev shook her head; he nodded his in response. "Fair enough, then. We know what we're going to implement differently – we'll carry on with the planning, the training, and the last few test runs. But we'll continue to hold off on seeing patients until we know how the results will be used. We'll be fine, make excuses as we go. We just need to hold our nerve," he added, more confidently than Bev could feel.

Chapter 15 – Tuesday 24th February

Lana's parents were comfortable on their sofa with their dog, Todd. He sprawled on his back, paws at their furthest reach, filling the gap between the two humans with limbs akimbo and usually-tidy jowls flapped back into a disconcerting grin. As Jen entered the room with a tray of mugs, his tail wagged enthusiastically, but Lana was pleased to see he didn't jump up to make a fuss: he was learning to stay calm.

"That was a lovely meal, Dad," Jen offered. "But once I've had this, I'll have to get Robbie home."

"No worries," her dad dismissed her apology. "It's so nice to see you both. Having you all together in the house like this is lovely. And Robbie is so good."

The toddler was sitting on the rug, surrounded by soft blocks and toys, happily playing. His hair was coming in thicker, now, and Lana's mum loved to wind his soft curls around her fingers, especially when she was reading to him, nestled on her lap. He was yet to utter his first proper words, so he was always the oblivious subject of great attention. Lana watched him through tired eyes; early morning starts had never suited her.

"That reminds me," Lana said. "How did you get on with the house viewings last night? Anything promising?"

"No," Jen replied firmly. "Neither was for us. I hadn't realised how soulless some of the new-build estates had become. I'm sure some of them are nice, but neither of those were. I have another viewing on Friday, though. It's one of the small semi-detached houses up near where Colin and Ailsa stay. It looks like it's been done up recently, so there wouldn't be much to do, and it's not too big, so I won't need to spend a fortune on furniture and fittings. I really like what I've seen of it online, and I've been to similar houses in the past - but I'm trying not to get my hopes up, in case it doesn't work out."

"What's for you won't pass you!" her dad advised firmly. "If you don't get something, it's because there's a better option on the way."

Lana smiled, knowing how frustrating this advice had been on previous occasions when she had been sure she already knew what she wanted, but she understood her dad meant well.

"Fingers crossed," she smiled.

"Fing!" Robbie cried, to everyone's delight.

Later that evening, Lana was lounging in her bedroom, reading her latest book and passing the time until Munro was free to chat. She and Bev had attended the opening committee meeting that morning, and now she was keen to share her news. She was struggling to concentrate on a lengthy chapter made dreary by the technical details of a sea battle, when her phone rang. Her heart rate accelerated, and she grinned as she answered.

"Hello!" she beamed, happily. "I've missed you; how has your day been?"

As Munro described a tiring day at work, and a fun-filled evening with Stuart, Lana relaxed into her pillows, reminded afresh of how Munro could so easily lift her spirits. She had never felt such unalloyed happiness simply from someone's company and attention, and knew it was a rare and precious thing. They quickly moved on to Lana's more eventful day.

"It was all a bit mad at the start," she admitted. "Lots of reporters and people were hanging around outside, but Bev beetled us past them. Thankfully, the building security team had everything in order, and once we were gathered in the room and people had helped themselves to drinks and chatted for a bit, it kicked off promptly. I think it went quite well. Bev feels that they're mostly sympathetic and they're not looking to persist with using the Bryant-Cargill legal agreements to circumvent the standard processes for handling mental health patients. Which is great. I must admit, I found it harder to judge, but we'll see. However, Bev still thinks it's going to take months to review all the information and have that formalised; in the meantime, she and Peter are still being pushed to restart their clinic. Peter is more wary of the outcome, so they're going ahead with planning another march to keep up the pressure – this time in London. They think it'll probably be early summer. Chris is worried that the UK government are using the "healthcare is devolved to Scotland" argument to wash their hands of this, but he maintains it's a bigger human rights issue, and everyone should be concerned at the precedents being set," she concluded.

"Okay," Munro replied. "It sounds quite positive so far, then?" he checked. When Lana agreed, he moved on. "I didn't know Chris was going to be there?" he asked, sounding a little too casual, a little forced.

Lana held a suspicion that Munro was unsure of the activists, and she wished he'd had the chance to meet them and see for himself how dedicated and driven they were.

"No, he wasn't there. He just mentioned it in a message."

"Oh! Oh, I didn't realise you'd kept in touch," Munro blustered. "That's nice. Umm..."

Lana waited, uncertain whether he was about to say more.

"Yes, nice. Umm," he repeated, "So, London? You'll be going down there with them again?" he asked.

"I think so," Lana answered. "If I can, and if we still need to make the point."

"That's nice," he repeated, yet again. "Sorry, I'll need to go. I have some work I need to do before tomorrow." He made a quick goodbye, leaving Lana perplexed and dissatisfied. She watched her phone for a moment, half believing he would call back. She thought through what had been said, and Munro's reactions. Doubts piled up into frustrations.

"Sakes!" she suddenly snapped, glaring at her phone.

"I'm not having this."

She pulled on her trainers and headed back downstairs, passing her parents as they were preparing for bed.

"I'm just going to pop up to Munro's," she announced. "Talk through today in person. I won't be too late," she advised, as she threw on her warmest coat and headed reluctantly out into the dark.

She marched angrily through the frosty streets, her anger not stopping her from admiring the fern-like frost patterns on car windscreens, and the diamante crusting on the black tarmac of the pavements. The streetlights above cast sinuous shadows on the ground as she passed beneath the trees and climbers which were being tossed by the biting wind.

"What a night to be out picking an argument," she muttered into her scarf as she approached Munro's house. She could see lights on downstairs but knew not to ring the doorbell and risk waking Stuart. She passed the front gate and slipped down the drive and into the back garden. As she reached the back door, she could see Munro sitting at his kitchen counter. His laptop was open in front of him, but he was holding his phone, a frown marring his brow, his teeth worrying at his bottom lip. She knocked, gently.

"Lana! I..." he tailed off as he saw the determined expression she bore.

"Tell me," she demanded, softly but unequivocally. "Tell me why you're not happy with me messaging Chris." She took his hand to soften the question, leading him back into the kitchen and perching on the stool beside his.

"It's not that, I just didn't know you were still speaking to him, that's all. I was surprised."

"No. No, don't try and sweep it under the rug. There's something wrong. Do you not trust me?" she braved.

"Of course, I do," he answered immediately. "I just... I don't really know what he's like, and Lind said -"

Lana cut him off there. "Lind? Why is what Lind thinks more important than what you already know about me? You either trust me or you don't, it shouldn't matter what Lind says. He's just somebody I'm getting to know because of the marches, he's no different to any other new friend or colleague. I'm not having this awkwardness every time I meet someone you feel insecure about, Munro."

Munro looked pained. "It's not that, honestly. It's just..." His mouth twisted, and he looked around his home briefly before visibly committing to the discussion with a reluctant nod. "I know I'm not ideal. I'm older, and I have Stuart to worry about. I work a lot, too. We can't go out whenever we want; I can't join you and your friends on pub nights. I couldn't even go to the march with you. Sometimes, I worry that you'd be better off with someone nearer your own age, someone free to do all the things you want to do."

"So, you think that the first single, child-free person I meet is going to be a threat?" Lana couldn't help herself retorting angrily. "Instead of talking to me about your worries, checking how I feel, you just assume I'll take up with someone like Chris? Munro, if you're worried about us, then talk to me – but don't decide for yourself how I feel about these things, and certainly don't make our lives more difficult because you're jumping to all the wrong conclusions," she added, breathlessly.

Lana took a moment to recover. The dishwasher hummed in the background, a car pulled into a neighbour's driveway, time passing as she considered what he had said. She realised that she could understand Munro's position, but she couldn't accept it. She also remained uncertain whether he was being entirely honest about it all. She sighed, and reached for his hand once more, tilting her head to see better into his eyes.

"Talk to me about these things. Please," she urged.

"I know. I'm sorry," Munro replied, daring to smile briefly before continuing. "I'm just not good at confrontation, but with you I'm even warier of it. I know how lucky I am to have you in my life, and at the back of my mind I'm always worried I'll mess things up. I do trust you, honestly. I know that you would have the courage to raise anything that you felt was wrong in our relationship, no matter what. And I'm not jealous that you're making new friends, either. I was just taken aback - I didn't know you'd stayed in touch. How was he with you, really? Lind has opinions," he winced.

Lana loosed a miniscule, almost bitter laugh, imagining what Lind had said. "He was fine. Lind is maybe right - or maybe totally over-reacting, who knows? - but it's totally irrelevant. I'm not interested in him. I'm happy with you, and Stuart. I love you. I don't want anyone else; this is where I want to be. Are we okay?"

He squeezed her hand. "Of course. Sorry I upset you. I'm just not good at talking about these things," he admitted again.

Lana decided to let it go, hoping it was unnecessary to press the point. "Hopefully we won't need to very often," she smiled.

Munro carefully tucked a wave of her hair behind her ear and smiled gently as he held her gaze. He kissed her, first gently then more confidently as she responded to his touch. Lana slid from her stool and led him to the bedroom.

Chapter 16 – Saturday 14th March

Jen linked her arm through Lana's and skipped a little as she stepped up the kerb and onto the mottled concrete pavement. It was a cold, blustery Spring day, and white cotton-wool clouds were scudding across the sky above them, heading out past the nearby hills on their haphazard journey from the North Sea over mainland Scotland.

"I'm stupidly excited!" Jen laughed. "I feel like I'm off on holidays, but all we're up to is a couple of hours of child-free furniture shopping and some lunch!"

Lana grinned in response as they weaved through the well-wrapped Saturday morning shoppers. "You've every right to be excited! You've been waiting for this for months now. I just hope they have some things that don't need to be ordered from the manufacturers, your moving date is so soon! Mind you, we have enough bits between us that we could manage to furnish the new place with loaners, if there is a long delivery time."

Jen had finally found her ideal new home but had been surprised at the rapid turnaround requested by the sellers. Suddenly, she was running around signing papers and arranging finances, while trying to plan their move and a catalogue of new furnishings. The house wasn't central to town but was only a twenty-minute walk away: Lana was pleased they were staying so close.

"I used to play in that street sometimes," she remembered. "My school friend, Beth, lived there. I used to think it was amazing, all those identical houses all in little cul-de-sacs, lined up like a comb. It all seemed very modern compared to our house, and the road was so quiet that we were able to go out and play on the nearby grassy area without her parents coming with us. It seemed like so much freedom. Well, apart from that grumpy dog walker shouting at us for distracting their dogs while they were being trained," she mused, plagued as always by her vivid memory. "It's a nice street, Colin is in the next road over and loves the area."

As they chatted, they approached the gleaming glass frontage of the local furniture store, and as they passed through its leaf-strewn double doors, they both took a deep breath. The mixed aromas of new carpets, leather sofas, and furniture polish was heady, and they giggled as they prepared for some serious browsing.

"So, what are we looking for?" Lana checked.

"A sofa and an armchair," Jen nodded firmly. "Nothing too bulky. I've got my table and chairs from you," she nudged Lana happily, "and the house has built-in wardrobes, but I need a bed and bedding, and I'll have a look at their cookware and dinnerware, see if there are any bargains," she admitted.

As they turned left, and focused on the living room mock-ups, Lana spotted an outsize blown-glass bowl that would match her lounge décor perfectly. When she read the price tag, however, she dismissed the notion; while she was building up her business, she needed to be frugal. She followed Jen towards the next set of displays; she would live vicariously through her sister's spending.

"Oh, I like this one," Jen called over. "But do you think dark purple would be practical with a toddler?"

"Is anything practical with a toddler? Other than mid-shade leather or plastic?" Lana laughed. "It certainly wouldn't stain anyway," she added, seeing Jen was torn between practicality and the beauty of the deep amethyst velvet of the ensemble she was admiring. "Let's see what else they have, don't rush to decide."

The sisters worked their way through the three floors of the store, toying with ideas and trying to visualise everything assembled in one small home. Jen relied on Lana's creative side to advise whether everything would come together, or be a hodgepodge of colours and styles. When they finally said their farewells to the salesperson, Jen's bank account was considerably reduced, but she was excited and pleased with her purchases – most of which were bargains for the quality of the stock.

"I wouldn't have been able to choose half of these things if I was still with Cal," Jen admitted. "He always wanted really conservative things: beige and grey dreariness," she added with regret. "It's so nice to choose things just for myself," she cheered visibly. "I can't wait to stretch out on my beautiful sofa, once Robbie is in bed, and sit back and smile at my own things in my own home."

Lana grinned back, knowing this was exactly how she felt about her flat, and realised with a jolt of surprise that she was just as excited to move back into her own little haven. They headed off down the main street, light in heart and step.

The glass-fronted gelateria and café was busy, but the waiter took them away from the families queuing for ice cream cones to the last free table in the window. It was always slightly chillier there, but well worth it for the view out onto the street, and the opportunity to spot passers-by of interest. They ordered wine and calzones, knowing they probably wouldn't need to eat again for the rest of the day, but happy to invest themselves in such a reliable indulgence. As they sipped water and waited for their drinks to arrive, a familiar face approached from a table towards the back of the room.

"Well, if it isn't the Knight sisters!"

Mr Miller was a favourite teacher from high school, managing to elicit an enthusiasm for modern studies which neither girl had expected. He was now retired and spent his time volunteering for many of the local charities, cementing his popularity in the small town. Now, he was shrugging his way into his winter coat while his wife and his sister waited patiently with a shared smile.

"Not long now before we'll be able to consign these to the wardrobe for the summer," he postulated, tipping his chin towards his chest as he fought with the buttons of his double-breasted duffle coat. "How are you both? And your parents? I hear you have a wee baby now, Jennifer?"

They answered cheerfully, remembering to enquire in return about his pair of elderly corgis, whose cheerful bopping gaits could often be seen at the nearby rock gardens. Before he replied, however, he turned to Lana.

"I read about your near miss with that profiling, Lana. You'll be glad you're out of that now! Especially with what's happening in Italy and Russia," he added, cryptically.

"Oh!" Lana couldn't hide her confusion. "I haven't heard anything about that – I've been busy with things here. What's happening?" she asked.

"They're setting some dangerous precedents," he replied ominously. "Have a look online! It'll end in tears, wait and see. There's a fine line between improving health over a population and outright cleansing, mark my words!"

"David! Don't be bothering the girls with your conspiracy theories," his wife scolded him. "He reads too much on the internet nowadays," she added to Lana, apologetically. "Come on, let them enjoy their lunch in peace."

As the group headed off to pay their bill, Jen raised her eyebrows at Lana. "I wonder what that's about?"

"I don't know." Lana shook her head. "But I'm not worrying about it now. I'll ask Munro later: he pays more attention to world news than I do. For now, I can see our wine coming, and I just want to enjoy our lunch. Now, what colour do you think you'll paint the vestibule, you said it was a bit too dark for your liking..."

"He might be right; it's hard to tell," Munro scrolled through search results uncertainly. "Pete could find out through his clinical connections in Europe, I imagine. But certainly, there are articles here claiming that the Italian government have allowed the police access to factorisation results during their checks, and that results are being taken into consideration for requests for IVF and some surgeries. There are rumours about results being made available to prospective employers, too, but they sound less reliable. The only thing I've seen about Russia is this blog, claiming they're doing factorisation testing of military and police candidates as standard - but there's nothing about how the results might be being used."

"That doesn't seem right," Lana offered, concerned. "We don't use clinical data for things like that here, do we?"

Munro disagreed with a tilt of his head. "Other health factors are considered when deciding whether someone is suitable for surgery, yes – they tend to be physical factors, but sometimes mental capacity is a fair question. And for employment, a prospective employee's health is often queried by larger companies – generally they just ask for written permission to contact the GP, although some places ask for medicals. HGV drivers are a good example. But there's a fine line between checking someone is fit to handle machinery, versus checking their mental state. But... it's plausible. It could be argued that knowing someone has a likelihood of developing depression, for example, would be vital if you were thinking of employing them in a role somewhere isolated. I can see the logic in some circumstances, but it could lead to discrimination if taken too far."

"I don't like it," Lana declared bleakly. "It's not just that factorisation could be flawed. It's not even that the testing could detect theoretical or potential problems that might never arise. It's the idea of using someone's weaknesses against them. These things should be used to make life better for people – not make it easier for society to cut them off from everyone else. We'd never agree to someone being refused life-saving care because they were diabetic or were a recovering alcoholic. I realise that some mental health issues, like psychosis, are scary for the public, but we shouldn't be condemning someone because they may suffer from it."

Munro agreed, reaching for her hand as he saw the determination and compassion in her gaze. But he also knew that there could be convincing opposing arguments. Yet again, he was relieved that Lana's results had been corrected before she could suffer any further impositions.

Chapter 17 – Sunday 22nd March

"Thanks again," Bev smiled. "Between last night's dinner and a fantastic breakfast, I've eaten better than I have in months!" she laughingly admitted. Last night, Lana and Munro had treated her to a wonderful meal of mixed tapas dishes served with a robust red wine, finished with a delicious homemade Crema Catalana. They had stayed up late, chatting and looking through old photos from Bev and Munro's student years; this morning they were all relieved to have avoided a hangover. Now, she and Lana waved off Munro and Stuart as they headed down the drive, Stuart chattering animatedly. He was spending his first morning in goal for his new junior football team, and his excited cheer had been infectious for the three adults.

"Let me help you clean up," she offered to Lana. "I think they used every pan and dish in the kitchen."

Lana laughed in agreement. "Yep, that's the norm for them. But I can't complain, not with a stomach this full."

Bev had been amazed when she came into the dining area that morning. Toast, butter, jams and marmalades had been staged in the centre of the table while Munro had ferried enormous plates of cooked breakfast from the counter. Gleaming bacon, sausages, and black pudding had clustered together, ringfenced by tomatoes, beans, mushrooms, not one but two fried eggs and a deliciously crisp fried potato scone. Bev had assumed she could never eat the whole plate, but had surprised herself, even finishing the meal with a slice of perfect white toast and lime marmalade. Now, she looked in dismay as she realised quite what a mess they had all made.

The two women busied themselves with the humdrum activity of clearing away leftovers and loading the dishwasher, chatting about Stuart and Munro. As Bev wiped the last few crumbs from the table, Lana dried her hands and stretched her back.

"What have you got planned for the rest of today?" she asked. "It's a nice morning, I wondered about borrowing my dad's dog for a bit, taking a walk along the beach. Do you fancy it?"

Bev was happily surprised by the offer; it would be the first opportunity she'd had to spend much time alone with Lana. "Are you sure? I have nothing on, and that sounds lovely. It'll do me good after all this rich food."

"Cool," Lana grinned. "We won't need the car, it's just down the road. We'll need to wrap up, though, it'll be blustery."

They picked up Todd from Lana's parents' house, and he pranced excitedly on his leash as they headed companionably through the town, towards the river and the beach. The skies were a stunning aquamarine as they passed other dog walkers, and the occasional dove grey clouds went scudding rapidly past them and out towards the North Sea.

Lana pointed out the local landmarks as they passed them, giving Bev a potted history of how the small fishing village had grown into a thriving seaside tourist town. Her enthusiasm for her hometown shone through everything Lana said, and Bev marvelled at the fondness her friend had for places and sights that could easily have been mundane to her. Bev shivered, and pulled her hat from her coat pocket, pulling it low over her ears.

"I can't wait for some properly warm weather," she grouched. "I'm sure I'm getting colder as I get older. Soon I'll not be able to leave the house without a ski suit."

Lana grinned mischievously. "I don't really feel the cold that much - especially once I'm walking," she countered. "My dad's the same, so I'm hoping it lasts. Saves on heating bills," she laughed. "My flat has big bay windows looking out over the river, and skylights in the upstairs. It would cost me a fortune if I kept it as warm as Munro keeps his place."

"Of course!" Bev realised, as they stepped down past the old stone castle and onto the sands. "You only just recently moved back in; I'd forgotten. How has it been? Is it nice to have some space to yourself again?"

Lana nodded wryly. "Oh, yes! Being at my parents' place was fine, but it's so nice to have all my things and some peace and quiet every now and then. Jen had looked after the place so well - there was nothing for me to sort out when I moved back in. And she bought me a gorgeous glass bowl I'd seen in a local shop as a thankyou: it was just sitting there, looking amazing on my dining table. It's been so nice," she reiterated, before looking thoughtful. "It is a little odd, though – I used to come home and spend a lot of my spare time on my furniture and other hobbies; now I do that elsewhere, for work! So, I have more spare time and less clutter in the flat. I'm far from bored," she grinned again, "but it's different living there this time around. Especially when I spend a lot of evenings with Munro and Stuart. My life and the things I love aren't all in the flat, if that makes sense?"

Bev smiled as she crunched her way over furrows of dried seaweeds. "I think so. Before, you didn't enjoy your workday, so home was a haven as well as the base for your favourite pastimes. Now you're happier and have more places in which you're happy. That's a good thing, but it also means that your flat isn't your main source of peace or solace." Lana nodded, seeming delighted that Bev had understood. "I'm glad things are working out well for you," Bev continued, surprising herself with her honesty. "Munro is so proud of what you're doing. Things seems to be going well between you two," she angled.

Lana nodded sincerely. "It really is. I've been so lucky with him. We hardly argue or anything at all. In fact, the only time we've really had a problem was when he was a bit put out that I'd kept in touch with Chris." Lana looked enquiringly at Bev suddenly. "He doesn't seem the jealous type, though. I don't think I have anything to worry about."

"Is that a question or a statement?" Bev asked with a smile. She didn't wait for a reply. "No, I doubt it. I've never seen anything like that from Munro. Ann was a stunning woman; while we were still studying, she had a far more active social life than we could. He never worried what she got up to or questioned her friendships. I think plenty guys tried it on, too – but he knew she would deal with it. I greatly doubt it would be jealousy or possessiveness causing a problem," she finally repeated.

Lana smiled sheepishly. "I didn't think so, but it's still a relief to hear that. I was maybe being a bit touchy about it. But I do think something is worrying him: the media attention makes him twitchy; he worries what people think of us."

Bev nodded thoughtfully. "I'll be honest - at first, I was concerned that he seemed to want to look after you too much. I couldn't tell if that was just a product of what you were going through when you first met, or if he had been unnerved by Ann's passing. But he seems to be a lot more comfortable with your independence now." She paused to let Lana correct her if she was wrong, then carried on. "It might just be a little insecurity about himself – he's a little older, more tied down. I imagine he'll get over it pretty quickly."

"He'd better," Lana giggled. "I'm at risk of poking him in the ribs if he gives me any more of that nonsense. Thank you. I didn't mean to grill you about him, or make you feel awkward," she apologised.

"God, no," Bev instantly dismissed what Lana had said. "I've been friends with Peter too long, it's great to talk about something deeper than work or sport."

They had now reached the old wooden groins, originally added perpendicularly to the beach to combat erosion. Rather than clamber past them, they headed up over the grassy dunes to the rock gardens which marked the end of the broad esplanade. Bev had never walked through these gardens and was surprised by the level of care the local volunteers took in tending the area. Between pretty streets and cottages, beaches, castle, parks and gardens, she found herself better understanding Lana's love for this area, and why Munro hadn't thought to move away in the years since Ann's death. On a Sunday morning such as this, it was peaceful and pleasing to walk through. She realised with a jolt that she was happier than she had been in months, perhaps years.

Chapter 18 – Friday 10th April

It had been one of those magnificently unseasonal April days – clear skies, only the lightest of breezes, and fresh growth had brought verdant new colour through the tired and worn greenery in gardens and verges. The sun had bathed Scotland in significant heat for the first time since September, and the thermometer had climbed rapidly from 10 o'clock onwards. Walking through town at a little after five in the evening, Lana spotted many sheepishly sunburned faces, knowing she was lucky that she always applied facial sunscreen as part of her morning routine. Working outside, sanding down an old pine dining table, she had shed her woollen jumper but had forgotten to protect her shoulders where they were bared by her vest top - now they smarted under the soft silk blouse which she wore.

She turned down the next side street and headed towards the river, glad she had wrapped up. When she arrived, the others had managed to grab a couple of small metal tables together, and were clustered in the evening sunshine, making the most of the warmth before the sun dipped behind Dundee and the chill drove them indoors.

"Before you ask," she pre-empted, "Munro is popping

down in half an hour. Laurie is watching Stuart for him," she grinned.

"About time, too!" Ailsa replied. "I'm fed up with Lind having all the chat about him," she laughed.

"I just turn up at their door every so often when I know Lana will be there," Lind demurred. "I'm not necessarily his favourite. Although - if we were going to be competitive about it..." they tossed their hair and looked smugly confident before laughing self-consciously.

The tables beside them were taken by quiet dogwalkers and practically dressed couples, but they didn't seem to mind the high spirits of the group beside them as they swapped their news. Munro arrived just as Lana was filling them in on the lack of progress made by the healthcare committee, and he grabbed a spare chair before settling beside Lind and Sanj to listen.

"So, it's all just dragging out in a ton of bureaucracy," she finally summarised. "I'd hate to work in that kind of environment; I don't know how Bev and Peter do it."

"Pete loves the political machinations side of it – Bev not so much so," Munro admitted. "I think some people just love being in the thick of things, even if that seems a bit alien to the rest of us," he added.

They were just about to move to a spare table indoors, when a figure stopped beside Lana. "Hello!" he interrupted them as they gathered their drinks. "Hope you don't mind; I was in the area and thought I'd stop in and join you."

The tone of voice made it a statement, not a question, and Lana could see the puzzlement in Sanj, Lind and

Munro's faces.

"Oh, hi!" she managed. "I hadn't realised..." she stopped abruptly, not wanting to seem rude. "Umm, everyone, this is Chris, from the protest group. Umm, we're just moving indoors."

Everyone took their cue and filed through the narrow entrance and into the seats beside Colin and Ailsa, who had grabbed the table as soon as it became free. The bar felt cosy after the fresh evening, and local art dotted about on the warmly lit walls depicted the town's fishing history as well as more recent views. The table was large, and Lana deliberately held back for Munro so they could sit next to each. The appreciative smile he gave her was one he rarely shared with others, a shyness and vulnerability differentiating it from the more professional veneer seen by most. Chris sat down beside Munro as Lana introduced him to the others, and Lind very pointedly took his other flank.

"So, what are you doing here?" Lind asked, sounding friendly but with no smile to back it up.

Lana was aware that Chris' appearance had already thrown the others. While she didn't want Lind to be antagonistic and spoil the evening, she admitted to herself that she wasn't certain she was happy to see him. He seemed remarkably comfortable with the situation, however, and after a further vague answer advising that he had been in the area and knew Lana and Lind were meeting that evening, he offered everyone a drink and headed to the bar.

Sanj raised an eyebrow. "I thought you'd only met that guy the once," he asked Lind.

"We have," they replied, looking unimpressed with

events and shooting Lana a look.

"I've been talking to him a bit, off and on," Lana interrupted to admit. "About the committee and things. I never would have expected him to turn up like this, though," she stressed. "I mean, I only said I was meeting Lind and you all for drinks, when he asked what I was up to this weekend. He must have just gone past by chance?" she added, hopefully.

Lind snorted. "Aye, or he's been trawling around the whole town like a weirdo," they retorted. "That's a bit stalker-ish, you must admit."

But Lana hated to judge too quickly. "No, he must just have been on his own up here, and we're the only people he knows in the area. I'm sure it was just a lucky meeting."

"There's certainly no harm in it, anyway," Munro backed her up, loyally. "The more the merrier," he quoted.

The evening was peculiar, however. Normally relaxed conversation was a little more strained, and Lana found herself missing Jen, who was enjoying her first relaxed weekend after settling into her new home. Chris spent most of the evening leaning past Munro to focus on Lana, blocking the others out of their conversation just as Lind had observed in Edinburgh. The table fractured, with Colin, Ailsa, Sanj and Lind having a fine time at one end, and Lana and Munro left to deal with Chris and a conversation dominated by his activism. By ten o'clock, Lana was resentful of the evening being spoiled, but still felt guilty for being unwelcoming. She turned to Munro.

"I'm done in. Shall we head home?"

She saw the dissatisfaction crossing Chris' face in the same instant she saw relief on Munro's. She turned to the others, seeing concern and worry in their expressions, too. It was a gut-punch of disappointment and guilt for her, as she worried that she had ruined everyone's evenings. When she and Munro shrugged their way into their coats and headed out into the evening, Lana could see Lind appraising Chris keenly, but washed her hands of any pointed questions that may be asked in her absence.

Munro took her hand as the door swung shut behind them. "Are you okay?" he asked, softly, as they started to walk along the riverside.

"I swear I didn't lead him on at all; there was no flirting or anything. Even his messages, I've just been answering his questions as quickly as possible then cutting off the chat. I just assumed it would peter out; I certainly never thought he would turn up here. Do you think it's okay to just head off and leave him there with Lind?" she fretted.

Munro couldn't help but loose a laugh. "Yes. In fact, it probably makes the point more eloquently than anything else you could have done. Might Lind perhaps be a bit sharp with him? Probably. Will he now know you're not interested in him? Absolutely, yes. He gambled, he lost," he summarised. "He does like the sound of his own voice, doesn't he?"

Lana sniggered, not only glad Munro felt unthreatened, but grateful she had someone with whom she could laugh off the evening. "Oh, yes. I guess he must assume that I'm political, because of everything. I just tuned out. He was so blatant in front of you, too - sorry." Munro shook his head. "I should probably apologise to Lind as well: they were right all along."

"Don't tell them that, we'll never hear the end of it," Munro laughed. "Laurie is staying at the house tonight – I wasn't sure how long we would be and she's happier in the spare room than heading home late at night. Shall we head back to yours?"

Lana grinned. "Hell, yes. My own place. It's been so nice this week to be back there. And it'll save us disturbing Laurie," she teased lightly with a tilt of her head. They picked up the pace and put the tricky evening behind them.

Chapter 19 - Monday 20th April

Lana gently kicked Munro's foot, desperate to maintain a straight face for the camera while he spoke.

"Yeah, it was a good evening - I thoroughly enjoyed hearing about how Chris recently managed to thwart Parliament's attacks on protestors' rights," he continued.

Lana gave up and stepped away from the laptop and into the hall, laughing under her breath until Munro had stopped his mischief. The group were waiting for Peter and Bev; Maria had joined the call just as Chris was introducing Munro to Martha, surprising her with the news that they had already met. Munro was letting Chris do all the explaining, and troublemaking in response. Lana hadn't heard from Chris since the pub, and she was glad, although still worried that she had mistakenly led him on.

As Bev and Peter connected from their clinic, Lana headed back to join the call, relieved the preliminaries were over. She was keen to hear the latest, as progress seemed to have slowed to a crawl. Bev led the discussion.

"So, I told you all about the last few meetings. I've now insisted that all the outstanding actions have owners and committed timeframes - everything is just dragging out too far. They think they have time, but we're being pressured to restart the factorisation clinic, and we're just not happy to do that until we know what the government will do with the patients' results. That decision has been punted over the wall to a UK-wide panel; some of the suggestions are crackpot, in my opinion." Seeing the concerned and puzzled expressions, Bev elaborated. "Adherence records for medication regimes could be considered during criminal sentencing. Diagnoses being checked during disclosure checks such as PVG and DBS. Firm diagnoses added to central records, rather than the current "potential for..." commentary. They're even talking about mandatory testing for candidates for police services and the military, that sort of thing. It takes our results - which we have always clearly noted as tendencies, rather than definite prognoses – and uses them as certainties with which to judge people. It's not right."

Peter was nodding firmly. "Ignoring the room for error we have recently uncovered with Lana; our results were never intended to be definitive. Our work was aimed at helping people understand and avoid mental health issues, not labelling people to limit their chances in life. We don't want to enlist or affect any more patients until we have this cleared up."

Lana looked to Munro, miserable. This was exactly what she had worried about. Munro spoke up.

"Lana and I were reading articles about how the factorisation results are being used in Europe, it sounds like that has been taken up here, too." Peter nodded in dismal agreement. "And our own government seems determined to undermine civil rights across the UK. I know it sounds paranoid, but I don't trust them not to subvert your work for their own ends. Can you continue to block them? And how long for?"

"We don't know," Bev answered. "We still have authority for now, but there's nothing to stop them handing ownership of the testing to someone else – or another clinic altogether. We only have that power while NHS Scotland grant it, and the rest of the UK don't have their own clinics."

Bev looked to Peter, who nodded. "We haven't told you yet, but... We've both had our salaries quite severely docked while the clinic remains closed. The rest of our team are okay, but – our superiors are losing patience with us. It may not be long before they side-line us entirely."

Munro dropped his head into his hands. "I am so sorry," he breathed. "That's appalling."

But Bev interrupted him there. "It makes our protests even more important. We need the public to be aware of what's at risk, and to be aware of what may happen if they agree to factorisation. Martha, how is the planning for London going?"

As they moved on to discuss arrangements, Lana sat back and took Munro's hand, distressed and worried by what they had heard. Munro stared out the windows into his garden, eyes unfocused as he thought through what they now knew. She knew he would be monitoring the conversation, but his mind was elsewhere; she wondered where.

"Who's coming to London, then, and when?" Chris asked.

"Lana and I will definitely be there," Bev answered, causing Munro to re-focus on the call. "Munro, are you still unavailable?"

"Unfortunately, yes. It's my mother's seventieth birthday. Lana can give it a miss, but I can't avoid it - her feelings would be too hurt," he explained.

"Maria?" Bev checked.

"I won't be able to make this one. Actually, I've been meaning to talk to you all about something; I've been putting it off, to be honest. You already know that I do some voluntary work... well, I've agreed to be the local branch director for the next few years. It's quite a commitment, but something I feel very strongly about. It's my chance to implement a lot of change that's been needed for some time - I'll have to give it some serious attention. But it leaves me with little spare time, and my family need me, too. I won't be able to help much more with your endeavours. To be honest, there's little I can do, anyway, now that the GP Committee are represented in your meetings, Bev. I feel bad, but it's time I stepped back."

Everyone understood, so despite their disappointment the rest of the conversation was mostly positive and congratulatory. They agreed their travel plan for the London protest and wrapped up the call. Lana and Munro went to the kitchen, the familiar pattern of making tea and toast together giving them time to process everything they had learned. As Lana poured boiling water into the teapot, Munro abruptly shook his head.

"Sorry," he muttered. "I'll be back in a few minutes, you get comfy."

Lana watched him go, perplexed, but finished preparing the tea and carried their things through to the lounge. She settled into the cushions of the sofa corner and relished her toast, hating to let it become cold and chewy. She was idly leafing through one of Munro's medical journals when he came back into the room. He looked markedly sheepish, she decided.

"So, I've done something a bit mad," he announced. "It'll take a bit of an explanation." He looked uncertain of her reaction, so she shrugged her palms towards him with a smile, in anticipation of what he might say.

"Have I ever told you about my grandmother?" he segued. Lana dropped her hands into her lap and shook her head, puzzled. "My mum's mother. She and I were very close. She was... well, her family were posh. Landed gentry, old money, sort of posh. She didn't much like my dad. It wasn't a snobbery thing - she approved of his background, his career, his politics. But she and my grandfather both thought he was a bit of a cold fish; it didn't help that he became more and more stern and reserved as the years went on. Dad... he adores my mum, but he struggles to show it in front of people. And with me... to be honest, I think he just couldn't work out how to be a good parent. Mum says that his own father was alternately distant and cruel, so he had no good example. My grandparents forgave him a lot, but they disapproved intensely of his attitude towards me." Munro paused, thoughtful, then shrugged. "Anyway, eventually Gran agreed with my mother that they would skip a generation of inheritance – she didn't want me to have to rely on my father for support at any point, and I suspect she also didn't want my dad to benefit from their family wealth. When Gran died, Mum received a smaller endowment, and the bulk of her estate came to me. It's quite a lot of money, Lana."

Lana was struggling with so much new information but didn't want to show it – she could see that this was hard for Munro. "That must have been so difficult for you – how your dad was with you, everyone discussing it so openly, the awkwardness caused by that decision. Did it affect your mum and dad's relationship?" she asked, curious.

"For a while," Munro agreed quietly. "But Mum put him right, said that it had never been her money, or his, and that if he loved her, he would accept her without a larger inheritance and be grateful for what they have. Thankfully, he did exactly that. They have plenty of their own money, they don't need anything. And it's not an issue now. I tried to pay them for the cottage, for example, but Mum wouldn't hear of it."

Lana could feel an unexpected fluttering of worry spiralling in her stomach but refused to give it thought. Munro was obviously uncertain about telling her this, so she wanted to know why he had done so at this stage. She asked, then waited patiently for his reply.

"I've just called Bev and Peter back." He looked up and directly into her eyes, startling her yet again with their warm depth and sincerity. "I've told them that I'll cover their salaries while we see this out, however long it takes. I'm sorry, I probably shouldn't have made that decision without talking to you first," he added uncertainly. Lana flapped her hands in gobsmacked dismissal of his apology, but he moved on immediately. "I owe them so much – not just as friends, but for how they've helped you, and for what we have together now. I couldn't leave them to struggle when they're trying to do what's right for a whole nation of people who will probably never know of their efforts. I'm sorry, I maybe should have told you all this before now, but... I didn't want it to affect how we are together. You work so hard, and are so proud of your independence, and here I am with so much, so easily. I didn't want to look like some posh toff."

"No," Lana argued. "Don't say that. You could take it easy, but you don't. You work hard for your patients, and for the surgery. I wouldn't judge you for having money. It's a bit of a shock, I'll admit. I just sort of assumed you owned this house because it was paid off when Ann died, or something.

I never stopped to wonder about anything else – you don't exactly drive a flash car or anything!" she laughed lightly. "To be honest, I was already a little wary of taking too much from you - when you offered that I could work from your garage, for example. I don't want to be that woman who gives up her independence the minute she's in a relationship," she admitted. "Anyway, it's totally up to you what you do with your money. I think that what you're doing for Bev and Peter is amazing, letting them hold to their principles without worrying about their bills. You're such a good man, Munro."

"No. It's Bev and Pete who are putting in all the effort – I'm just carrying on as normal," he demurred. "Are we okay? This doesn't... bother you or anything?" he checked.

"No, course not," Lana rubbished. "Now, eat your toast. It's annoying me congealing there," she laughed.

Chapter 20 - Tuesday 21st April

Lana crept down the hall and through the front door, carefully manoeuvring the heavy wood in its frame to avoiding waking Munro or Stuart. It was early in the morning, but she had woken filled with a restless need for solitude, so she had left a note and pulled on the running gear she kept amongst her overnight things. It had been a chilly, damp, drizzly night, but she knew it wouldn't be long before the mist on her exposed skin was a blessing rather than a curse. She zigzagged along quiet and tree-lined roads, grateful for the lack of traffic or other pedestrians. Once she had warmed up thoroughly, she sprinted up a particularly challenging hill, enjoying the burn in both legs and lungs as she pounded out her pace and let her erratic thoughts settle and surface as they wished. Since the previous evening, she had known something was bothering her, and she hoped that silence and exertion would clarify it for her.

Was she bothered that Munro was wealthy? That didn't feel right, but she certainly wasn't against the idea of helping Bev and Peter, either. So, what had he said to discomfit her? She was perhaps a little put out that he had hidden his wealth – but then, had he? They had never discussed finances, but he had always made it clear that he wouldn't let her lose her home when she lost her job, for example. She had just assumed that he meant he could cover a couple of months mortgage payments for her, without giving it any more consideration. She briefly wondered how much wealth Munro really had but felt an immediate shame at her nosiness: it was none of her business, she resolved. She thought again. Did she care that he hadn't told her before now? She pondered that awhile, playing with the idea. He didn't want to affect their relationship, didn't want to sound like "a toff", he had said. He knew how independent she was. Did he think she might be a gold-digger? No. She had been clueless about his money, had already refused a number of offers of financial and practical help with her business. She rolled the problem over and over in her mind, hoping to wash out a reason for her adverse gut reaction, but failing. Munro's money shouldn't affect them, she was sure. It didn't bother her.

She shook the introspection off, and turned downhill again, towards the river. The drizzle of rain had eased, and the clouds had cleared. The sun was just about to start rising, and the lightening aqua tones of the sky reflected on the glassy, rolling waves out to sea. The wet pavements shone cleanly in the streetlights and growing dawn, and she lengthened her stride once again as her route levelled off. She thought ahead to the protest being planned in London, and realised she felt reluctant to meet with Chris and Martha again. Chris' behaviour at the pub, and his comments in Edinburgh, had contrived to put her off him. She felt a stab of guilt at the thought: it was her own fault for not making it clear that his interest wasn't reciprocated. She certainly wasn't going to let a slightly awkward situation put her off such an important event.

She ran on, past an empty park and dark-windowed

homes, down onto the esplanade which followed the sandy dunes of the beach, then around the castle and the communal green and playpark as she headed towards home. But as she neared the old fishermen's cottages, she veered off back towards town, and increased her pace with a determined expression. She needed to talk to Lind.

"Lana! Is everything okay?" It was unusual for Lana to turn up unannounced, never mind wet, sweaty and breathless. "Come on in." Lind grabbed her by the arm and tugged her through the doorway, tightening their silk robe. "My neighbours will be talking about me again," they laughed.

"I'm sorry for just turning up, but I needed to run some things past you. I thought I'd catch you before work – I didn't wake you, did I?" Lana worried.

"No," Lind replied easily, heading through to the small kitchen. "Don't worry. I'll make us some tea and breakfast; sit down. What's up?"

There was a thump from upstairs, where Lind had converted the loft space into a large bedroom and en-suite. It was their private space; Lana knew that even Lind's lovers didn't make it past the original, ground-floor, boudoir-styled spare bedroom. She raised her eyebrows in question.

"Umm, yeah. I've been meaning to talk to you about that," Lind added, flustered. "Umm, Sanj is here," they finally blurted, the blush spreading across their neck and cheeks adding to Lana's amazement.

"Oh!" she replied, for a second unsure of what else she could say. "I can come back later if it's not a good time?" she managed.

"No, this must have been important. So long as you don't mind him being here?"

The uncertainty and vulnerability in Lind's demeanour pierced Lana's heart, and she felt a swell of caring for this friend she had seen too little of recently.

"Of course, I don't mind! Oh, Lind, I'm so happy for you." As Lind's grin finally re-appeared, Lana laughed her relief. "I'm so happy for you both," she carefully re-worded. "I'm just sorry I didn't know; I've been so busy recently."

"No, don't apologise. It's fairly recent, and we've been keeping it quiet. We finally spoke properly after that Chris turned up at the pub that night. Sanj was worried he'd come to see me – imagine him being jealous! Anyway, we didn't want to make a fuss until we knew how we really felt."

Lana gathered Lind into a tight hug, breaking off abruptly as Lind pulled away in a dramatic show of indignation and disgust. "Sorry. I forgot for a second," she looked down at her damp running outfit in dismay.

"I'll forgive you," Lind retorted, turning to the kettle as it finished boiling. "Just don't ever do it again. Hang on," they advised with a lifted finger, before stepping back out to the bottom of the staircase. "It's Lana!" they called. "She knows you're here, come down and get some breakfast when you're decent!"

"Sit down and tell me everything," was Lind's command, and Lana complied, finishing her rambling tale with a plaintive, "So I know all the things that aren't bothering me, but not what is! It's niggling at me." She smiled appreciatively at the scrambled eggs and toast which Lind had just served up, her stomach rumbling its approval.

"Thank you, these look delicious."

To her surprise, it was Sanj who spoke up. "What started it? The call with the others, or the conversation with Munro?"

"Definitely Munro," she replied. "The other discussions were depressing, sure, but not worrying at me like this."

"Do you think Munro having money will change your future together?" Sanj continued.

Lana sat back and pondered. "I don't know," she finally decided. "We haven't talked much about the long term," she admitted. "Just ideas for holidays, what I want for my business, that sort of thing. We did talk once about me moving in with him and Stuart – when I was thinking about moving back into the flat. But we both agreed it was too early to plan anything, for us as well as Stuart. I still like my own space, and they need time together, just them. We thought maybe in a few years, we'd reconsider. I don't know if his having lots of money would affect that, though."

"Okay," Sanj continued. "So, in a couple of years, if it came back up. What would you think, knowing he had wealth?"

"I don't think it would make much difference. I would still pay my way – I'd sell or rent out my flat, I'd have my business or a job. I think I'd be more inclined to keep our finances separate, though, now that I know. I guess I wouldn't want to be seen as a freeloader," Lana shrugged.

"All sounds quite sensible to me," Lind interjected. "So why the panic?"

Lana stabbed at her scrambled eggs in frustration. "I don't know. I just feel like things are different now... out of balance, somehow." She screwed her mouth as she thought. "It's like what Chris was saying in Edinburgh." Unnoticed, Lind rolled their eyes. "He was saying that because Munro was my doctor, I would automatically see him as an authority figure, and none of my decisions about him would be unaffected by that. I disagreed – I don't see Munro like that at all. But... with this latest thing... I feel like the scales have tipped somehow. I'm this young flibbertigibbet, without even a proper job, and with no savings, just muddling my way through life. And Munro is so much more a proper adult, with a proper job, and a proper house, and God knows what in his savings accounts." Lana looked exasperatedly at Lind, who was choking on the mouthful of tea they had taken just before Lana called herself a flibbertigibbet. "Oh, you know what I mean!" she exclaimed.

"Not really," Lind laughed. "Sorry, sorry," they appeased. "Lana, this is nothing to do with Munro's money. It's about how you see yourself. What you're doing with your furniture and crafts is amazing, everyone thinks so. Don't let your insecurities and what that arse Chris thinks taint how you feel. Don't dismiss it!" Lind exclaimed as Lana shook her head. "He's obsessed with you – turning up out of the blue when you're with friends, that's classic manipulative stalker-y behaviour. You're letting him weasel his nasty way into your thinking. Everything he says is biased bollocks, Lan, and you should know that without me telling you," they concluded.

Sanj seemed to agree, nodding minutely. "It sounds like you have no real problem with Munro at all, Lana. You're just worried that you'll seem less well-suited to him because you don't have investment funds or something. Which, when you put it like that..."

"Is a bit mad. Yeah, you're maybe right," Lana muttered, thoughtfully.

"I mean, if I moved in here, would you think I was just after Lind's house and savings?" he continued. "No? Exactly."

Lana smiled reluctantly, letting go of the tension she had been carrying since the evening before. "You know, I think you might be right. Thanks."

"Yep," Sanj answered smugly. "You're lucky I was here. You should come to me for all your advice in future," he added, ducking as Lind playfully flicked his ear.

Chapter 21 – Saturday 23rd May and Sunday 24th May

"I don't like this. Not at all."

Lana looked to Bev, her face mirroring the alarm Bev felt in her gut. A crowd of people jostled past them, their shouts incomprehensible in their anger, scarves up over their faces and placards stripped of their boards, revealing the bare two-by-four beneath. What would normally have been a bright and modern street of stores now seemed oppressive and claustrophobic.

"I know," Bev replied. "I was worried enough when Martha said the crowd were too riled for us to talk, but it's getting worse. I'm worried there's going to be trouble; this is nothing like Edinburgh." She fumbled with her phone, trying once again to reach either Chris or Martha, and stepped to the side of Lana so they were both pressed up against the shop windows behind them.

"Neither of them will answer," she muttered through teeth ground together by her frustration.

"I've spent weeks trying to convince Munro this was

perfectly safe, teasing him that he was being a middle-aged alarmist. If this goes wrong, I'll owe him such an apology," Lana admitted with a grimace and a glance up and down the street. "Should we turn back the way we came? We're meant to be meeting the others towards the end of the march, but I have no idea if these crowds are following the proper route or not. Do you?" she asked, hopefully.

Bev was equally uncertain as to what was best, but tried not to sound as panicked as she felt. "I'm not sure. I know where we are on my maps, and I know where we were going, but the route map Martha sent won't load on my phone. We can get to the end easily enough, or we can go along with this group, but I'm not very comfortable with that," she admitted.

"Let's try and head back onto more main streets then head towards the endpoint," Lana decided. "It will hopefully be quieter there."

The two women wove through the crowd to the next large junction, then headed east. But here the crowds were hardly moving, and they found themselves pushing their way past tightly packed clusters of men and women. Many of them were drinking; it seemed like all of them were angry. Bottles were being thrown aside as they were finished, and Bev had to duck as one was launched into the masses by the man beside her. His face was florid, his eyes coldly calculating; he leered at Bev as she scuttled out of the way.

"Come on," she muttered to Lana, "we'll take the next quiet turn. This is a powder keg," she prophesied.

Behind them, there was an almighty crash as a shop window was somehow smashed, followed by jeering and laughter from the mob. Now, it felt like they were not just surrounded by the braying and roaring of justifiably angry people, but by a mindlessly furious multitude. Bev and Lana shared a look of true fear. They pushed their way through the crowd, occasionally seeing other alarmed faces as they struggled to get back to less tempestuous waters. As they cleared a corner, Bev glanced down a narrower side-lane, and saw what she hoped was a quieter thoroughfare. She grabbed Lana's hand and pulled her towards it, breaking into a light jog, already anticipating the relief she would feel when they arrived in safer streets. But just as they passed the last brick-faced building in the pend, their exit was suddenly and alarmingly blocked by a wall of masked men armed with batons, bottles, and debris. The two women skidded to a halt in front of them.

"Oh, shit." Lana uttered Bev's thoughts as her own.

They stepped aside, huddling into the filthy wall and gutter, desperate for the men to pass. Their luck, however, had run out; they were soon surrounded. There was no ringleader, no one to appeal to. Bev's instinct to try and calm the situation was wasted – her futile show of empty hands slapped aside. Lana's instincts differed: she adopted a defensive stance, both fists clenched and raised unconsciously to her shoulders as her usually attractive features somehow melded fear and defiance.

"Please! We're protesting, too! We just want to go past!" Bev attempted, to no avail.

Two of the men already had Lana pinned against the wall, her own outstretched arms used to hold her in place. As they leered, another man stepped forward and pulled a short but menacingly sharp-looking knife from his hoody, and Bev could have wept.

Clarity comes at such times. Clarity of feelings, priorities, and regrets. Clarity of memory as each sound and scent of the scene in front of us is recorded in crystalline light. Time slows, allowing details to be picked from even the most complex of dioramas. As Bev swallowed down the acid which had bubbled up into her throat, she noted the small scar beneath a young man's shaved hairline, jagged and badly healed. Beside him, someone needed to trim his ear hair, and the absurdity of this observation rocked her. As the knife was raised and brought up to Lana's face, Bev watched the blade, somehow seeing in it the reflection of the sky above them where it broke the monotony of brickwork and guttering. In her next breath, she saw the widening of Lana's pupils as fear stretched her senses and overrode her will to fight. Each eyelash on her friend's eye was clearly visible as the knife paused below it; Bev felt a despair she had never previously known. She abruptly realised that all the noise was now far in the distance – this group were silent, watching their prey intently, Lana's desperate pleading the only voice to be heard.

The knife-holder broke his silence, the recognition in his grim sneer somehow worse than anything else so far. "Well, if it ain't the famous mad bint from Scotland," he crooned as he leaned into Lana's pallor. "A bit far from home, ain't you? That doctor you're shagging ain't here to save you this time around, is he?"

Bev watched Lana's eyes widen even further in horrified despair as she realised her predicament was being made even worse by the minor infamy she and Munro carried. Lana was stammering, trying to explain herself somehow, trying desperately to diffuse the tension – but Bev found her mind blank, found herself helplessly watching events play out as if it was all just another TV drama. She wanted nothing more than to be far away, rescued somehow from this nightmare and transported home by a miracle.

The surreal tension of the moment was abruptly broken by another group entering the alleyway. Threats and curses began to be exchanged immediately, but Bev couldn't take her eyes from Lana's face until the knife was safely away from her skin and held out towards the newcomers.

"Come on!" bellowed a familiar voice, and there suddenly was Chris, somehow amongst them all, tugging on Bev's arm, breaking the frozen tableau. She, in turn, grabbed Lana, and they skidded down past all the men and out into the street.

"They'll take care of them, don't worry," Chris continued, as if he was talking about cleaning up after a children's party. "We need to get you two back to your hotel. This has all gone to hell, there's riot police further down the route and everything," he concluded.

Bev clung to Lana, and they hurried after Chris as he dragged them down streets filled with protesters and police, somehow navigating them past the worst of the violence. Gobsmacked gratitude filled Bev's thoughts, as she processed their unlikely escape - and even less likely hero. Bev could hear Lana's breath, ragged and tearful, and knew it replicated her own; they held each other as they ran and stumbled after Chris' lead. They finally came out onto quieter streets, far from the protest, and slowed their pace.

"What the hell just happened?" Lana demanded, fear morphing into fury.

"No idea," Chris disappointed them. "Factions, maybe? Troublemakers, definitely. But there's loads of them, it's completely out of control. I can't get hold of

Martha – it was pure luck I found you two. We should be fine now, but you should get back to the hotel - there's no way to be sure this area will stay unaffected. Do you know where you're going from here?" he demanded.

Bev put aside her panic, fear and anger, focusing purely on the needful. She knew where she was, knew tube stations and main roads, but she didn't trust anything at this point.

"We're getting into that taxi," she declared, pointing across a road. "And you're going nowhere until we're safely in it."

Four hours later, Bev and Lana sat on their respective beds in their hotel room, wrapped in monogrammed hotel robes and staring disconsolately at the TV.

"I can't believe this. It's just a nightmare." Lana sounded close to tears again, but Bev could provide no solace: she felt exactly the same.

"Look at them," Lana continued.

Bev focused once more on the images streaming onscreen. The protest had somehow devolved into a full-blown riot the likes of which London hadn't seen for years. Riot police were struggling to contain and control the disruption, and reporters relayed rumours of the army being deployed to assist. One scene was played time and time again, police on horses charging dense crowds as they threw flaming bottles towards a police barricade. Bev found herself unable to correlate their planned protest with the savagery she saw on screen: that was not her fight, those were not her people.

She was shaken from her reverie by a sharp knock at the door and went to answer it with a puzzled frown.

"Chris! We didn't expect you..."

Bev ran out of words, not wanting to apologise for their robes, not wanting to invite him in, uncertain as to what he could want. He took the decision from her hands, though, breezing past with a grin.

"The publicity we're getting from this is amazing!" he crowed, throwing himself onto the bed beside Lana. "Everyone will be paying attention, now! They'll not be sweeping any of this under the carpet!" he continued, oblivious to the looks of horror the two women were sharing.

"You can't possibly think anything about this is good!" Lana exclaimed before Bev could speak. "This is horrific! This makes us all look like thugs!"

"Oh, we'll issue a statement decrying the violence, don't worry, that will cover our backs. But this will be all over the media. It's our chance to get our point across to a much bigger audience."

Lana had moved away from him, and was perched on a corner club chair, pulling her gown belt tight. "I have no idea why we would want to be associated with this at all after today," she declared. "We're trying to make a peaceful, democratic, educated and rational point – not cause a riot."

Bev listened to them debating the point, letting the arguments wash over her as she watched the scrolling footage on screen, surprised to find that she agreed partly with both. Yes, she hated the fighting and looting – but if it opened an opportunity to get their reasoned arguments across to more people, she wouldn't waste that opportunity. She hoped Lana wouldn't judge her as harshly as she was condemning Chris.

Early the next morning, they huddled on the chilly, windswept concourse of King's Cross station, watching excited families head towards Platform 9¾. They had ushered Chris from the room as soon as was polite, choosing to order room service and absorb the expense rather than heading back out to eat. This morning, they were left deflated and disgruntled, and Bev could see that Lana was anxious, her frown and chewed lip betraying her occasional cheery comments.

"I'll be glad to get onto the train and away from here," Bev admitted. "How are you doing, really? You don't need to pretend to be okay, I totally understand," she added.

Lana paused, then shook her head disconsolately. "I don't know," she admitted. "The shock of it all is wearing off, but... It's like my thoughts have nowhere else to turn. I keep reliving those minutes in the alley; it's like flashbacks, they come out of the blue. Realising what was happening - feeling so helpless - thinking that he would cut me. Worrying that it was all my own fault for not staying home, for talking at the other march, for being in the papers again. Then the sheer relief and gratitude when Chris turned up with whoever those other people were. I try not to think about all of that, but then I just remember sitting in that room, watching the news, realising what a mess it had all become. Then Chris turning up again, turning out to be just..." she searched for the right word. "Nasty," she shrugged helplessly. "So, I try not to think about that, either. But then

I worry about what will come next, what the reaction to all this will be," she admitted. "Munro is being amazing, keeps messaging me, telling me I'll be home soon, and everything will be okay. But I just can't seem to stop thinking and thinking about it all. About what could have happened to us. About what will happen next! I mean - will it be okay, Bev? Will this not make things worse?"

Bev nodded her understanding. "A never-ending loop of dismal thoughts, with no comfort. The flashbacks will be just that – from the trauma of being attacked and the fear of what could have happened. If that goes on too long, let me know or talk to Maria about it. But certainly, it's not in any way your fault! You've done nothing wrong - and you've stayed out of the media as much as possible. Don't fall into the trap of blaming yourself for their actions, Lana." She waited until Lana nodded her agreement before changing tack. "What's your biggest fear? What are you most worried could get worse?" she asked, knowing that talking would help Lana most.

"That we'll be held responsible because we organised the march," she admitted. "Will the police blame us? There was so much damage; I dread to think about the people who might have been hurt," she added, tears welling in her eyes.

"No, Lana, no. None of that is our fault. The police will know that these were factions we couldn't control. Our protest was legal and organised – they hijacked it. It's the fault of the people who were attacking others, looting shops, using our march as an excuse for violence. They're in the wrong, not you. Don't blame yourself," she repeated. "You were a victim of them, not a perpetrator."

Lana was nodding her head. "I know that, really - logically. But it doesn't stop me feeling like this today. I'm sorry."

"Don't be," Bev shook her head. "I understand, honestly. Come on, it's time to get on the train. Let's pick up some breakfast and some snacks; something to eat will shore us up."

Chapter 22 – Thursday 28th May

Lana's phone buzzed again, the vibration shifting it minutely on the glossily polished dark wood coffee table. She tried not to look, tried to continue watching the movie Munro had chosen to distract them both, but she could feel her temper rising as she quietly jumped to conclusions. She shut her eyes and grumbled.

"If that's him again, I'm telling him where to go," she ground through her teeth.

Munro lightly rubbed the back of her hand with his thumb and leaned his head over to gently touch the top of hers. "You've told him you're busy; replying to him might just encourage him."

She gave up with a shake of her head, sitting forward to check her suspicions. "Yep. This time, he's apologising, and hoping we're okay. What a chancer."

Chris had pestered her constantly throughout her journey north on the train, messaging to ask how she was, trying to convince her that the protest had not been the disaster she thought, wanting her to commit to talking to the media about the day. Disgusted and disinterested, she had first made her point clearly, then stopped replying, then stopped reading. His response was as disproportionate as it was dramatic: turning up at her door on the Monday evening as she came home from her day working in her father's garage. He had veered erratically from rational discussion of their efforts together, to a frighteningly proprietorial and jealous entitlement to her time and attention.

"I'm so sorry," she turned back to Munro. "I feel like I've really messed things up this time."

"Lana, you've done nothing wrong," Munro stressed. "He's acting completely inappropriately. He has no business harassing you, no business coming to your home, no right to demand you listen to him, no cause to be angry with you for avoiding his calls. I'm just glad he didn't get into your flat, and that your neighbour came to check what the raised voices were about. If they hadn't got rid of him by threatening to call the police, who knows how it would have escalated?" he worried.

"I really didn't mean to encourage him. And now, everyone is worried about me, and my neighbours think I'm hanging around with criminals or something. He's still inundating me with messages and calls. And then all this fuss in the news..." she lamented.

The news had quickly turned from the rioting to the details of the protest, at first blaming the organisers, including Bev and Peter. By the Monday, the journalists had somehow found out that Lana and Bev had attended, and their focus once more included the friends. The articles and gossip published online and in newspapers affected not just them, but all their families. Chris was overjoyed with it all, wanting to use the publicity to further their causes; Lana hated being tarred by the rioters' actions and wished that the march had never happened.

"What if this negatively impacts the committee discussions?" she worried. "Or worse, Bev and Peter are blamed for it all?"

Munro shook his head. "It was clearly not their fault. Let them fight their own fights – you don't need to worry for everyone, Lana. We're doing what we can for them, and you're already doing more than you need to with regards to the committee and everything. There's only so much any one person can do," he reminded her gently.

"You've been right all along," she concurred regretfully. "About me getting too involved, about the media, about Chris. I'm sorry I didn't listen. You must be so frustrated with me." She felt a hint of hot tears gathering behind her eyes and looked away to calm them.

"No. Never," Munro vowed, sitting forward and claiming her gaze. "I wish I'd been wrong. I wish that things had gone smoothly, for you and for everyone. I hoped I was just being cynical. Don't ever regret having faith in the goodness of people, Lana. That confidence and trust you have is a wonderful thing." Here, he paused, watching her carefully. "How are you really doing, after what happened to you and Bev in the street?"

Lana let loose a sigh, nodding gentle agreement. "I know. It's still bothering me, and that's making me less... able to deal with all this. It could have been so much worse. I keep reliving it, wondering what could have happened. The fact that it's Chris who got us out of that situation – versus how he's behaving now – it's confusing for me. I was so frightened, and I'm so grateful he came along with those others and helped. I feel ungrateful when I judge him so harshly now and ignore his calls. But since then, he's really shown his true colours. Rationally, I know I need to avoid him – but it's all just a bit of a muddle for me," she admitted. "Hopefully, once all the fuss has died down, I'll be able to put it all behind me." Munro smiled a small smile, smoothing her hair back from her face. "I'm not going to any more protests, or meetings with Chris and Martha, though," she announced. "I'll still attend any committee meetings Bev wants me to, but no more protests."

"I'd be surprised if Bev doesn't feel the same way," Munro added. "I'll support you, whatever you decide. But, in future, I want to be there with you – if that's okay," he asked.

"Oh God, Munro, of course. But I'm pretty sure I'm done with it," she concluded.

Later, as they cleared away their mugs and switched off the lit lamps dotted across Munro's ground floor, Lana sighed, and shook her head.

"What's wrong?" Munro stopped in front of her and took her hand.

"Another evening wasted on worrying and fretting," she answered, shoulders slumped. "And now it's late, and we need to be sensible and get some rest for tomorrow. Let's not do this again," she announced. "Let's put this behind us."

Munro watched as she first smiled bravely for him and then reached for her hoody and shoes before sitting down on his hall bench.

"Okay," he agreed readily. "But don't worry too much – we have plenty of time ahead of us. And... if it ever becomes too much bother, having to head home at the end of the night... Or if you aren't comfortable being alone, for any reason... Well, you're welcome to stay here any time. Stuart is so happy when you're here. He's been asking if you're going to come and live with us. So, I don't think we need to worry too much about him anymore, is what I mean. And I would love to have you here. Umm, it would be up to you, at your pace, if that makes sense," he trailed off, looking embarrassed.

Lana felt a swell of love and gratitude, marvelling once again at her good fortune to have found such an open, generous and caring partner. "Thank you," she replied with a soft kiss. "That's so good that Stuart is adjusting to us so quickly. But it's certainly not just up to me. Staying here more often – or even moving in - that's for both of us to think through. And decide carefully, rather than just reacting to circumstances. With all this trouble going on, I want to keep that away from Stuart; he's still the most important thing in all of this. We should talk about it more another time, yeah?" she checked.

Munro still looked uncertain, but they reluctantly kissed their goodbyes. Lana headed out into the darkened night, lighter in heart and calmer in mind, and resolved to clear up her messes before making any decisions that could affect Munro and Stuart.

Chapter 23 – Friday 29th May

The early summer sun was slowly lowering into the west, bathing Jen's back garden in syrupy light. Bumblebees busied themselves around a length of lavender which divided her small patio from her lawn, and a blackbird sang out stridently, letting all and sundry know of her neighbour's prowling cat. Todd snuffled his way along the obvious perimeters, occasionally stopping to lay claim to this new territory. Jen watched him warily, clearly concerned for her new flowers, while her mum smiled wryly.

"He'll not dig them up or damage them," she reassured the world at large. "Our garden has survived so far."

Jen, Lana and their mum were comfortably ensconced in some of Jen's new garden chairs, soaking up the sunlight and shedding the workweek worries. Robbie was toddling on the lawn, happily pushing a rattly toy lawnmower while his grandad kept a watchful eye and paced out measurements in the furthest corners of the flat grass.

"These chairs are so comfy," murmured Lana. "Such a bargain, too. Who really cares that they're last years' stock, I wonder?"

"Not me," laughed Jen. "I never thought I'd get a new house and new furniture then spend our first family evening sitting outside, but it's glorious."

The weather had suddenly become full summer, and Jen's plans to cook a housewarming meal for her family had rapidly become drinks and takeaway. Lana watched her dad frowning as he turned in a circle, working out the path the sun would take through an average day.

"What's he up to?" she finally asked.

"We're going to bring Robbie one of those climbing frame swing sets with a slide," her mum replied proudly. "Just a little one. Two doors over were going to get rid of it, but it'll last until Robbie is big enough for something more adventurous. Your dad wanted to bring it tonight, but I said he had to check with Jen how she wanted things laid out."

"Lana! Jen! Look!"

Stuart came running over from the small vegetable patch, hands loosely clasped together.

"Caterpillars!" he exclaimed. "Dad says they're murder for lettuces, but it's worth it for pretty butterflies," he went on, opening his palms and revealing two inch-long wrigglers for the women to admire. "Will he be here soon, Lana?"

"Yep, maybe another half hour or so," she advised, checking her watch. "Go fetch them a nice-looking leaf and we can keep them in the shade until he gets here."

She turned, catching her mother in an expression blending both amusement and pride, followed by a cheeky grin.

"I didn't expect to see both my girls doing such a good job of parenting quite so soon," she admitted to her daughters. "Although you're not really girls any longer. The years have passed me by somehow," she rued. "It's so nice to all be together again for the future – I'm so grateful to be here with you both."

Lana was surprised by how touched she was and took her mum's hand briefly. "I'm glad we're all here together, too," she agreed. "It's nice that you're getting out more, Mum."

Jen looked worried at this turn in the conversation, but her mum smiled broadly. "Robbie has helped. I can't be sitting in the house when he wants to have fun out and about! And I couldn't miss seeing Jen's new house. I should come to yours more often, too, Lana," she added quickly. "But the stairs are such a struggle."

Lana waved away her mum's explanation, neither wanting nor needing it, then turned to her father.

"Well?" she demanded. "How much play equipment are we talking about, that it will cover the whole lawn?" she laughed.

Her dad came to sit down, grabbing his cold soft drink gratefully. "I reckon we should put the playset in the south-west corner," he advised. "Your neighbour's trees will provide some shade on hot afternoons. If you don't want to keep the vegetable patch, I can turf it over for you – or put up a wee summerhouse or something? You've got the garage for storage, so you shouldn't need a shed."

"Peter, let Jen work it out for herself," his wife chided him gently.

Jen smiled appreciatively. "No, that's okay. I'm not sure what to do, Mum. I thought it might be nice to grow a few things, maybe? It could be fun for Robbie. Easy things, of course. I even wondered about a small greenhouse - your tomatoes are always lovely, Dad."

"They take a lot of looking after and watering, mind. But I can do that if you're away with work or on holiday," he offered. "You get ones that build up against a wall, you could put one over there," he pointed towards Jen's north boundary and the high breezeblock wall which would protect her garden from the worst winter winds. "It would have to be glass, though, plastic would just rip and blow away. I made that mistake once, never again. I wonder..." With that, he headed back off to stand before the wall, feeling it's blocks for warmth and prodding at the ground with his toes.

Jen turned to Lana, offering her more wine from the bottle which had been sitting in the cooler at her feet. As Lana passed her glass, Jen peered at her over her sunglasses.

"So, how are you doing? Really?" she asked, bluntly.

"I'm fine, honestly," Lana dismissed the question quickly, not wanting to spoil the evening.

"Bollocks," Jen countered, to a stern look from her mum. "You can't possibly be. You were under enough pressure as it was, without being attacked in a riot and then gaining a stalker." Jen spotted Lana's grimace and waited patiently for an answer.

"Well, yeah. But I've thought about nothing else all week, and I'm sick of it," she explained. "Sick of it going round and round in my head. Sick of worrying. Sick of everyone worrying about me – sorry. And sick of not being able to change any of it, anyway, no matter how much I think about it all! And the fallout of it all has me so worried. Trolls on social media saying that we should be finding anyone unstable and locking them up, things like that. Why do some people have to be so awful?" she grimaced, keeping her voice low for the children's sakes.

"You've been through a horrendous experience," Jen summarised. "At the end of a stressful year. It's normal to still be processing it all, I'm sure. Do you think you need counselling or anything?"

Lana shook her head. "No. I think I'll be fine. I was so lucky it didn't end up worse than it was – that's what I'm focusing on. I've been going out, just like normal. I even walked home alone last night, and I didn't feel frightened or anything. I don't think I ever want to go to another protest, or be amongst massive crowds for a while, but other than that I think I'll be okay. I'm being sensible, honestly," she added, hoping to reassure them.

But Jen wasn't to be deterred. "And this Chris," she continued. "What will you do about him?"

"He's gone quiet, thankfully," Lana sighed, sipping her wine. "Hopefully he's realised where he's gone wrong and will drop it. I shouldn't have to see or hear from him anymore, anyway: Bev and Peter are dealing with their group. Other than helping Bev with the committee there's nothing else I absolutely have to do."

"Thank goodness for that," her mum declared. "You've done your bit. It's up to politicians and doctors, now. They'll settle on a sensible solution, I'm sure. Whatever they do, they won't catch me doing any of their tests, for sure!"

Jen looked unconvinced, however. "It depends on what's forced on you, though, mum. Testing could become a prerequisite for benefits, or employment, or anything. It's not just trolls," she corrected Lana. "There are a lot of organisations calling for reform, saying that the public should be protected from the mentally unwell the way they used to be before "Care in the Community" became a thing. I was reading an article about it, some of the arguments are quite persuasive on the surface. I don't buy them," she rushed to confirm, "but some of the people I've met at the nursery, for example, are in favour of it. If enough people become convinced, who knows what might happen?"

Lana groaned her dismay. "Oh, don't, it's not worth thinking about, especially on such a beautiful evening."

However, her mum stopped her there. "Actually, Lana, there's something else we should tell you," she advised. Lana felt her stomach fall slightly, and put her glass down on the tabletop, anticipating tough news.

"Those reporters were back," her mum continued. "They've been told – probably by that Chris - that you weren't just at the protest, but that you were caught up in the riot. They were asking us if you were involved in the violence, and if we thought you were emotionally stable. We put them right! But... Well, they do have all the details of what you told the clinic, dear. They showed us the notes about some of the bleak thoughts you have sometimes – about people dying, bad things happening. They asked what we thought of it. We told them we were proud of you for baring your worst fears like that, and being so open to the testing, but that we certainly weren't worried about you at all. They went away quite unhappy, to be honest," she chuckled at the memory. "I think they were hoping for a different reaction. But we thought you should know they were digging around again."

"Oh God, Mum, I'm so sorry..."

"Don't be!" her mum interrupted her. "You've done nothing wrong, not in any of this. Just... be careful from now."

Lana nodded, resigned. "I will. I wish I'd never got involved in any of it. Or that I'd listened to Munro and kept a lower profile. He was right to worry," she admitted.

"Now, enough of all that," her mum pivoted. "Munro will be here soon, it's a beautiful evening, Jen's new house is wonderful, and we're all together. That's more than enough joy to combat all that gloom. What do you girls fancy to eat tonight? If we let your father choose it'll be fish and chips again, and I would rather do something spicy," she grinned.

Lana sat back with a smile, grateful for her mother's pragmatism and cheer, and her ability to seemingly switch off worries when she needed to. She knew it was a skill she had not yet mastered but determined to practice it for everyone else's sake.

As they planned and plotted the rest of the evening, Lana watched Stuart and Robbie playing together, marvelling at how well Stuart handled the much younger child. They were passing a ball back and forward, Stuart doing all the running to make up for Robbie's lack of co-ordination. He delighted the youngster by throwing himself to the ground to try and catch the ball, and shouting "Goooaaaal!" when it slipped past his fingers. When he shot up from the ground and hurtled towards the garden gate with a grin, she knew Munro had arrived, and felt a warm swell of love and elation.

"Happy weekend!" she called to him, raising her glass in a toast. "There's a glass here for you, but grab another bottle from the fridge, and the menus from the counter. Jen gets to choose seeing as it's her treat," she winked with a laugh.

Later, when the night was chill and everyone safely at home in their beds, Lana nestled against Munro, and warily told him of the journalists' visit to her parents. He sighed in dismay, then kissed her lightly on her hairline.

"You were right all along; I'm sorry I didn't listen," she concluded.

"Don't be; I wish I'd been wrong. If they publish any of it, we'll sue the hell out of them. They'll know that, so it's only worth doing if it will make them more money than they'll lose. That's incredibly unlikely, thankfully, so I wouldn't worry about it. And don't ever change, not because of people like that. I would hate for you to become as fearful as I am, to become a worrier. Your ability to see the best in people, to trust, to care – that's a rare thing, Lana, and I love it. I love you. Don't ever change," he repeated, his voice thick and warm with affection and sleepiness.

Lana stroked his shoulder where she lay, comforted and secure, knowing he would be with her throughout whatever was foretold.

"I love you, too, you marvellous man," she breathed softly, smiling as the last tension left his face, and his breathing slowed to sleep.

Chapter 24 – Saturday 27th June

Bev eased her pace a little as she exited the busy road and turned off onto the public footpath. She had chosen her route for maximum distraction and least traffic, accepting the greater distance it would entail as penance for the more pleasant walk. As she had headed along past Cramond Beach and the Silverknowes golf course she had considered simply stopping and trying to enjoy the day on her own, but at heart she knew she couldn't let her friends down. They were meeting at one of the trendier eateries near Stockbridge, and the table had been booked for weeks. The lunch had been intended to be a special occasion – Munro and Lana celebrating a rare weekend without Stuart, Peter bringing Sophie along to meet them for the first time, mid-afternoon food and wine. She knew her latest news had spoiled any festive atmosphere, but the others had insisted on gathering anyway, still wanting to share their weekend with her and provide a distraction from her worries. She should have been getting a taxi to the bar, glammed up and perhaps even in dress shoes, but she had needed to get outside, hoping that sunshine, fresh air and exercise would somehow enervate her and make her more palatable company. Her trainers and sundress would cause little comment in Stockbridge, anyway.

The sun shone warmly as the path bypassed the back gardens of mature suburban homes, and she was startled by an enormous heron as it veered down into one long, narrow, heavily planted plot. She hoped that the owners had sufficiently protected whatever pondwater had attracted its attentions, remembering her father's many tirades against his lost carp and the greed of prehistoric wading birds. Brambles tangled through the trees to the other side, and she smiled as she thought of the fruits they would bear by autumn. But where would she be by autumn?

Yesterday, she had been called once more to see her superiors, their patience finally having met its end. She had been accused of embarrassing the health service, of failing to protect patients and their data, of displaying a clear conflict of interest, and of refusing to follow their direction in re-starting the analysis of patients. Her position was untenable.

That word was stuck with her now, spiralling through her every thought. If this had happened a month previously, she would have been shocked, furious, determined to fight her cause. But now? After all these weeks of warnings and worry, she accepted their decision with bitter understanding. She agreed: her position was untenable. She couldn't continue to fight their dangerous decisions while she was on their payroll. She shook off her anger, determined to make the most of the day, and move on. She had time now to think, to plan, and to decide her best way forward.

The path continued towards the south of the city, but Bev turned off and headed towards Comely Bank and Stockbridge, realising she had plenty of time and easing her pace accordingly. The midday sun was hot on her shoulders, making her glad of the sunscreen she had applied after her shower. This road was busier, and she took reassurance from the simple normality of people passing her with shopping bags and mobile phones. Life went on, and so would she. By the time she was approaching the end of her journey, she was in the best frame of mind she could muster.

The others were already there, Peter making introductions while the wait staff delivered paper menus. Lana and Sophie had both opted for more casual outfits, too, making Bev glad she'd stuck to form and avoided anything too restrictive. She slid her sunglasses off and through her hair as she cut past the other already-busy tables.

Everyone rose to hug her briefly, even Sophie, who muttered, "Pete told me what happened: I'm so sorry. He's furious," she added, looking Bev directly in the eyes to check she understood how carefully she had chosen the adjective.

Bev mustered a smile, surprised at how easy the moment was. "No, don't worry. I need some time to think it all through, but... Well, I'm not surprised, or even particularly sad about it all. It'll work out."

Lana was watching her carefully, her perceptive gaze searching Bev's features for clues.

"Well, we're here if or when you want to talk about it. But if you'd rather put it aside for now, we'll not be the ones to pester you about it, either," she asserted with a typically gentle, lop-sided smile.

"Thank you," Bev smiled ruefully. "I don't want today to be about this, you know? So! How was Stuart when you dropped him off?"

Munro grinned. "Oh, fine. Mum had the kitchen ready

with all the makings of a chocolate fudge cake. He was in heaven. Lana and I got short shrift," he laughed. "Mum is looking forward to their week together while Laurie takes her holidays, and to be truthful, we didn't tell him we were coming through to see you all today. He can't be jealous of what he doesn't know about!"

"Where are you staying tonight?" Sophie enquired.

"The Bonham," Lana offered. "They had a good deal on, and it's easy walking for wherever we end up. There's a great little café nearby for breakfast tomorrow, too. Always about the food, me," she laughed.

"Good point," Bev agreed, grabbing a copy of the menu. "What are we all having? The last time I was here I had the celeriac tart starter, and it was amazing," she suggested.

Their meals were delicious, and they lingered over wine and desserts and cheeses, only leaving the restaurant late into the afternoon. Bev felt a peculiar discord, tipsily leaving a restaurant into afternoon sun reminding her of their occasional post-exam celebrations as students.

"Who fancies a walk along the Water of Leith to the West End?" Peter suggested. "We could get another drink or something once we're there?"

The group headed up through the back streets to join the Water of Leith walkway, the sun's heat quickly becoming stifling whenever they were without shade. They all felt the drinks they'd had, but in the holiday atmosphere of late afternoon sunshine they felt carefree and unembarrassed by their cheer. They took their time, gradually splitting into two clusters, Sophie talking animatedly with Peter and Munro, while Lana hung back with Bev. Bev knew she was being given space to talk if she needed it, surprised to find that she was ready to reveal a little more of her feelings.

"I'm not really okay," she finally broke her silence. "This all feels... false. Fake. Like I'm pretending for everyone," she mourned.

"I wondered," Lana admitted. "To be honest, I'm not sure I'm okay just now, either - and I've had peace and quiet since London, not the hard time of it you've had. It's a beautiful day, but I still feel slightly on edge because we're out amongst other people. That's mad - I mean, what could possibly happen here? So, well," she stumbled to explain, "I think that what we both went through at the protest was bad enough. What's happened to you since... Losing your job, everything you've worked so hard for all these years – and so unfairly, too – it must be overwhelming." She paused before rephrasing the question Bev had posed while they were leaving London. "What's the worst thing about it for you?"

Bev laughed bitterly. "That one's easy, I'm afraid: I agree with them. I can't carry on working there, not when they're going to force us to test patients and potentially condemn them to discriminatory treatment. But I'm conflicted about it. I still feel possessive about it all: that it's my work, my processes, my clinic, my staff. I feel like they're stealing it all from me... and it's so unfair, Lana. I don't know what on earth to do next. I'm relying on my savings, and the money Munro has been sending me. After all this, can I just get a normal, humdrum, clinical job? Would anyone even hire me? I have no idea what the future holds. I'm trying to be positive, to appreciate having some time to decide... but I feel so bitter as well. I hate it."

Lana sighed. "I think I understand. What will you do this week? Won't you feel a little lost without work to go to?"

"Oh, hell yeah. I haven't done anything but work for so many years now! I feel so sorry for Pete, too. He has to carry on with it all, despite this. We're so used to working through everything together, so it'll be odd for him, too. I don't know what I'll do. I wondered about taking a proper break, going someplace quiet for a bit, taking it easy. I don't know if that's just delaying the inevitable, though."

Lana nodded, then subconsciously quoted Munro from the year before, when she had needed time and space in a similar but also very different position.

"Actually, we might have the perfect thing," she smiled. "The cottage. It's perfect for taking some time out, to decompress or whatever. There's no one there. It would let you forget about it all for a bit, then come up with a plan."

Bev stopped, turning towards her friend as relief and gratitude bubbled erratically across her thoughts.

"That would be... amazing," she managed. "You're right, it's the perfect place. Are you sure Munro won't mind?" she checked.

"Munro won't mind at all," Lana stressed. "He's already said that – if you'll let him - he wants to carry on covering your salary until you have something else. We're here for whatever you need, Bev."

Bev sobbed, a graceless, guttural manifestation of everything she was struggling to contain, and grabbed Lana into a savagely tight hug.

“Thank you so much,” she whispered, as she let go of the younger woman’s embrace. “You two are amazing. This makes things just a bit less of a yawning unknown,” she managed to smile through her tears. “And for me to be able to force a smile right now just shows how much of a difference it will make,” she acknowledged with a broader and more natural grin. “Come on, let’s catch up with the others and see if they fancy another drink just yet.”

As they gained on the slower threesome, they quickly realised that Sophie, Munro and Peter were also deep in a more serious conversation. Munro was nodding thoughtfully, and had just asked, “So what do you think you’ll do?”

Sophie tipped her head unhappily to one side, a resigned half-smile flitting across her profile. “I think it’s too good an opportunity to refuse. It’s my dream role, and they’re offering me benefits and progression I just couldn’t make here. And I would be within an hour’s drive of my sister and her family, now that they’ve moved. I love it here – and things are so good just now,” she looked back to Peter and took his hand, “but I’d be mad to turn it down.”

Peter nodded ruefully. “You must take it; everyone here will understand.” He looked to Lana and Bev. “Sophie is going to take the role in Ottawa. After she spoke to them last week, they’ve improved their offer and broadened the scope of the role to cover everything she wanted. She’ll be heading over there in a few weeks,” he explained.

At first, Bev didn’t know how to respond. She knew this was great news for Sophie, but it was another blow for Peter, and she felt for him. She had been so sure this relationship would go well for them both, but long distance was a difficult thing, especially for two such busy professionals. Congratulations seemed harsh under the circumstances, but it was still absolutely the right thing to do.

"That's fantastic news for you," she commended Sophie. "It's not easy to negotiate exactly the terms you want! And such an exciting move. I've never been to Ottawa, only the west coast and the Rockies. Do you know the city well?"

Gratitude for her reaction was clear in Peter's gaze, and Sophie grinned, pleased to turn the conversation in a more cheerful direction. They moved on through the summer heat, the spirit of the afternoon changed again from one of commiseration to one of celebration.

Chapter 25 – Saturday 4th July

"It's like being abroad!" Ailsa slumped onto the sand beside Lana, fanning herself with her hands. "I can't keep up with them anymore," she laughed. "Do you need some help here?"

The others were all more competitive, however: they were keeping the game of beach volleyball going until there was a clear winner. Lana was lining a hole in the sand with large pebbles, for use as a firepit, and Lind was soaking up the sun in hip-high cut-off jeans, a bikini, and a chiffon kimono, huge sunglasses obscuring their expression.

As Ailsa started collecting more stones, Lana squinted at Sanj, Colin, Munro and Stuart, who had been drafted in to replace Ailsa. "They won't last much longer, either. That's the third time Colin has eyed up the drinks cooler," she observed. "Dad's dropping the food off soon; I'd better get the fire started."

The beach was broad at this point, and the tide was far out. They had chosen a safe spot, sufficiently out of the way of everyone else, but just below the high tide line so that any leftover ashes would be washed away over the coming days.

"This is your first turn at staying until the fire has cooled, Lind," Lana noted. "How are you feeling about that?"

"Oh, don't worry about me!" Lind exclaimed. "I have all sorts of warm clothes stashed in the car, and plenty drinks and food to keep us going. Sanj wanted to bring sleeping bags, but there's no way I'm trying to sleep the night on the beach. We'll stay until the wee early hours and make sure everything is safe, then walk home with the dawn," they laughed. "The car will just have to wait until tomorrow evening!"

"It gets pretty chilly later on," Lana warned. "And once the last of the wood is gone, it takes hours for the coals to cool enough to leave safely. It doesn't give off nearly as much warmth, but it's still too hot to just soak and bury. It's a pest."

"Yes, yes, Mum!" Lind half-joked, their raised eyebrow forming the classiest of mild reprimands. "I'm not a complete berk, you know."

Lana grinned. "Uh-huh?" she teased briefly. "No, I know, honestly. But I just remember hating it the first time I stayed back while the others all headed home for hot showers and their beds. The next time, I had a hundred layers of clothes and covers," she giggled.

"Here they come," Ailsa laughed, as Lana started the fire. "I reckon it's time to crack open the drinks."

Stuart threw himself down into the sand beside Lind, announcing that he was exhausted and definitely deserved a fizzy drink after all his running around. Munro smiled fondly as he pulled a can from the cooler and popped it open for his son.

"Agreed," he grinned. "But don't be fidgeting and covering Lind in sand, or you'll be banished into the dunes," he warned.

It didn't take long before Stuart had bored of his inactivity, and as he wandered off to watch the sand martins perching on the tall dune grasses, swooping through the air to feed, and dotting in and out of their roosts, the adults settled around the fire, watching Lana slowly and carefully build it with logs as they savoured their cold drinks. The breeze was light, and fairly steady, so no one was too overwhelmed by smoke.

"While Stuart's little ears are elsewhere," Sanj opened, "what's the latest with the committee you were helping, Lana?" he asked.

"Ooft," Lana pulled an expressive face. "God knows what will happen there. I'm out of the loop now, and they've punted Bev. So, it's just a bunch of politically minded careerists making decisions in isolation."

"The usual, then," Sanj interjected. "No say for us, and they'll no doubt be protected from the consequences somehow, whatever they decide. Our government really is a farce," he opined.

The others nodded, turning back to Lana for her thoughts.

"Yep," she agreed. "It's such a mess. The Scottish government are waiting for the NHS committee to advise how the results of the analysis should be used, and who should have access to them. But, in the meantime, they've insisted that Peter restarts the clinic in Edinburgh. They'll be using the revised, much safer process – and he's going to monitor all the patients' results, try to ensure that no one would be persecuted, depending on what the committee decides in the long run. There's only so much he can do, though: if someone is already unwell, he'll have to diagnose them and treat them, and that will be on their medical records to be used however government sees fit." She paused briefly to think. "And then the UK government is heading in their own direction. We've heard that they plan to pass the health committee's guidance to another board of ministers to decide the UK policies – and are opening their own Factorisation clinics without involving Peter or Bev. That's what has happened in other countries," she admitted, "but... I guess I just don't trust them. And what happens in the wider UK will have repercussions for us all, as usual. And God only knows what they'll decide about Compulsory Treatment Orders. It's a mess," she repeated, in dismal summary.

Ailsa laid a hand over Lana's knee, in sympathy and support. "Colin and I were reading an editorial piece in one of the online Sunday papers," she advised. "It sounded mad – they were trying to use the protests and riots as examples of the sort of thing we could expect if there weren't tighter controls of people with mental health conditions! They were totally conflating the issues, misrepresenting the facts. At first, we just thought it was some awful, mad, extremist columnist... But you should have seen the comments section, it was appalling. It wasn't just bots, either: properly large numbers of real people were seriously commenting that they thought anyone unwell should be sectioned - "to protect normal good folk"", she quoted. "Like they wanted to go back to the old asylums from Victorian times," she shuddered.

"They'll just be the vocal idiots, as usual," Lind asserted. "Real people never think that way. Well, apart from my family," they added bitterly.

"I don't know," Munro countered. "It's amazing how opinion can be swayed when people are scared and uncertain. They forget that the "others" they're talking about are really their neighbours, their families, their hairdressers or whoever. Look at the fallout of Brexit, the upswell of intolerance and xenophobia which both sides of that political movement caused. We're still paying the price of that as a society," he mused. "I wouldn't be surprised by an upsurge in fear and a kneejerk reaction – especially if politicians and the media decide to encourage it."

"Oh, don't," Lana found herself pleading. "I can't bear the thought of it. I can't bear the idea of people being frightened to seek help because they'll be persecuted as a result. I hate the idea of people's mental state being used against them, like that. Don't they understand that anyone can end up unwell, whether some testing says it's likely or not? And that sometimes the testing is just wrong?"

Munro moved closed to her and put his arm around her shoulders. "Try not to worry too much," he advised. "There are a lot more sensible people in the world than we sometimes think. I shouldn't have been so gloomy," he apologised, with a gentle kiss to her hairline.

The others agreed that sense would prevail, and after a while Lana moved to add more logs to the fire, stopping only when she heard Stuart call out, "Here comes the food! I want sausages, Dad!"

Lana smiled once more, cheered by the simple joy in his voice and face as he raced to help her father with his bags. "I'll not put any fresh logs on just yet, then," she decided. "Coals are better for cooking!"

For a short time, they were all pleasantly occupied - welcoming Peter, setting out wipes and sanitiser, and opening bags of food and paper plates. He had prepared the makings of grilled cheese sandwiches, and there were burgers and sausages, vegetable kebabs and thin chicken skewers for everyone to cook over the coals, as well as rolls, salads, and plentiful cakes and snacks. He had brought the large frying pan and barbecue baskets Lana kept especially for campfire cooking, and the shared bustle of the moment raised her spirits as much as the thought of warming, delicious food.

Later, when the last scraps were finished, and Lana's dad had taken Stuart back to her parents' house for a bath and a sleepover, the three couples lounged around the campfire, replete and relaxed.

"Hopefully in a year or two, Jen will be able to bring Robbie without worrying about him too much," Lana mentioned, still regretting her sister's decision to keep the toddler at home instead of letting him join the sleepover. "I feel like she's missing out: this is just the perfect evening."

The sun was dipping slowly into the west, painting the river and skies in myriad sunset hues. The beach was surprisingly quiet this far from the town, only the occasional dog walker disturbing the seabirds at the shoreside. The breeze had dropped, and the sea haar which often marred the evenings of warm days had taken the night off, leaving perfect conditions for sitting outdoors.

"I wonder what we'll all be doing in a year or two," Ailsa mused. "Lana, you'll be hiring apprentices to help with your business," she suggested loyally.

"Munro will be preparing for Stuart to go to secondary school," Lana teased an alarmed Munro.

"Hah!" Lind retorted. "You'll be right there with him; we're amazed you two aren't living together already!" they added cheekily.

Munro smiled wryly at Lana. "It's not for want of me asking," he answered. "But Lana is not to be rushed!" he advised.

"Nope," Lana agreed, perfectly happily. "Everything in its time. But what about you two?" she countered, raising an eyebrow at Lind and Sanj. "What does the future hold for you both?"

"Another beer!" joked Sanj, reaching into the cooler hopefully.

"I wouldn't mind a bigger house," confessed Ailsa. "More room to maybe have a family in a few years."

Lana watched Colin's eyes widen, and a smile slowly grow on his shy features.

"Do you mean that?" he asked, sounding as tentative as they had ever heard him.

"I think so," Ailsa replied, seriously. "Not just yet..." she warned him. "But I don't want to be too old, either," she added.

Everyone was now watching them carefully, aware of how important this moment was to them both, not daring to interrupt them.

"I thought you would want to be married first?" Colin's timid question took Lana's breath away.

Ailsa's eyes were shining as she held his gaze. "I would, if I was asked."

Lana buried her face in Munro's shoulder, happy tears suddenly coursing down her cheeks.

Chapter 26 – Wednesday 15th July

Bev looked around her kitchen in dismay, unable to believe the number of piles of laundry she had brought home from Munro's cottage. She had spent a little over two weeks there, luxuriating in the silence gifted by the solid stone walls, and the distant rumble of waves on the shore as she sat at the doorstep and read novels in the sun. She had walked, slept, read and eaten entirely to her own schedule, ignoring her future concerns for the entire first week, then quietly contemplating her options once she felt able. She had seen only walkers and distant neighbours for most of her stay, only twice venturing into the busier town for supplies.

Now, she was home, her calm resolutions were wavering, and she could feel herself hankering for her old routine. She shook off her dismay and busied herself with chores. She had quite the "to do" list to cover.

She was considering her options for dinner, when her door buzzer sounded. Seeing Peter outside, she grinned and let him in. Spotting that his hands were full of food containers, she fetched tableware and glasses, and was just opening a bottle of Malbec when he came through the open door.

"Welcome back!" he grinned. "If you're not hungry, I'll just eat it myself," he teased.

"You know me too well," Bev laughed. "I was just about to go rummaging in the freezer, hoping for leftovers. Oh, now this is much better," she exclaimed, uncovering portions of rice, salads, pitta bread and chargrilled lamb and chicken. "Heaven! I've been cooking for myself for weeks, you know," she laughed. "Tell me everything. How is Sophie settling into Ottawa?"

"Oh, she's loving it. They've put her up in an immaculate apartment complex in the downtown area, while she finds her feet. We had a great first week exploring together, and I got the chance to meet her sister and her family – they're really good people. She started her work on Monday - she says everyone has been really welcoming, and things look promising."

As Bev beamed her congratulations, and shared out plates of food, Peter poured the wine. "It certainly sounded like you were having a good time away, too" he ventured.

"I really did," Bev admitted. "I hardly ever take time off, never mind going someplace so quiet, on my own. But it was just what I needed – peace, privacy, a complete change of scenery and pace. It's lovely down there. I wasn't fully aware of that when I was there to see Lana - it was so different in the winter compared to the beautiful weather I had. Well, apart from the three days of torrential rain and howling gales," she corrected herself with a smile. "But even that was spectacular, watching the weather chase its way along the far hills."

Peter was smiling at her, and raised his glass in a toast. "Here's to us both finally having a holiday, then!" he laughed, then sobered. "Sorry, I shouldn't make light of it all. I still can't believe you're not coming back into work. It's not just that I miss working with you, having you there to share it all with - I just can't seem to get over being angry at how you've been treated. I'm not sure I can stay there - not carrying this grudge," he admitted.

"Oh no, Peter," Bev pleaded. "It's bad enough that I've been pushed out of our programme; I'd hate for you to be out of it, too," she protested.

"I know – and I don't really want to drop everything we've worked for here, either. But it's just not the same without you, and..." he paused, looking uncertain suddenly. "I don't want to upset you even more, but – there's another opportunity that's just come up, that I'm seriously considering."

Bev was stunned. She had been so focused on her own removal from their work, and what the future might hold for her, that she hadn't even for a moment considered that Peter might walk away from their efforts. A brief, bitter thought flashed before her: he didn't even need a new job! He had one - surely that was unfair! Horrified at her reaction, she forced a smile, and promised herself she would never let him know how she had felt.

"I had no idea! That should be exciting news – don't look so worried! Tell me all about it," she managed, before hiding her face briefly in her wine glass. "Let's eat, and you can tell me everything."

Peter's smile of relief was reward enough for her dissembling, as he forked together rice, meat and vegetables, and started to talk.

"You already know that some of the Canadian provinces have been interested in picking up our Factorisation for some time – they just haven't had the funding in place yet. Well, when I was out in Ottawa with Sophie last week, I offered to meet with their Medicare team, just to catch up and see where they were in their journey. When I explained why I was there... Well, Bev, they want me to head up their programme there. They would fund my move and sponsor the process from what they call "landed immigrancy" to citizenship, if I wanted that in the long run. It's a fantastic opportunity to start again with our programme - somewhere more supportive - and make a real difference."

Bev could barely breathe, barely believe what she was hearing. Peter was leaving, would live thousands of miles away, would be working with their beloved programme in a fantastic new area... without her. She was so happy for him, but her heart and soul were hurting in a way they never had before. She couldn't swallow the mouthful of wine she had taken, could feel hot, sharp tears prickling behind her eyes, threatening to spill at any second. But Peter – her Peter – was watching her minutely, and she couldn't bear to hurt him.

"Oh my God, Peter," she ground out. "What an opportunity for you! I can't believe this has all happened so quickly, it's amazing!"

"Bev," he stopped her, in dismay. "No, Bev – I haven't agreed to it. Not yet. Please don't be upset. I want you to come with us, Bev. I spoke to them: they'd love to talk to you. They approve of the stance we've taken here! We can do this together – it's our opportunity, not just mine."

And now those tears did spill, and Bev lowered her glass to the table and pushed aside her untouched food. Her breath juddered through her as she sobbed, hands trembling as she covered her face.

"Ignore me! I'll be fine in a minute. It's just a lot to take in," she explained, wiping the traitorous tears from her cheeks and laughing off her embarrassment. "What am I like?" she demanded, semi-seriously.

The discussion paused, as they both sat and calmed themselves, not knowing quite what to say.

"Thank you," Bev eventually stressed. "I can't thank you enough for that, Pete. It means so much to me that you want me to be part of this with you. Part of me would love to agree, to walk away from this mess we've been enmired in here. But I can't; I'm sorry. I need to stay here, to find a way to sort things out, somehow! I think you should absolutely go - but to start a new life, with Sophie, with a better balance in your lives. My path lies here, though, Peter," she concluded, reaching across the table to grasp his hand.

"Are you really sure? I can't see what difference either of us can make here anymore. A new life would be good for you, too, surely?" he argued.

"No. No, I'm totally certain," Bev shook her head. "But you are going to be amazing!" she stressed. "You'll make such a difference to so many lives and have your own wonderful life with Sophie. Oh! How do your parents feel about this?"

Peter looked ashamed. "I haven't told them yet. I wanted to talk to you about it first. I wanted to see how I felt after talking to you. I think I want to do this, Bev."

"Then you should! And you'll have no regrets. And there are flights, you'll still see everyone often enough. I've always fancied a holiday to Canada. Oh, well done, Pete!" She raised her glass in a toast and glanced down at her plate. "Cheers!" she smiled, more genuinely this time. "But we really ought to eat this before it's wasted. It's a sin to waste food, you know," she grinned.

Later, once Peter had left to head back across town, Bev padded to her kitchen and opened a second bottle of wine, throwing caution to the wind. She was still stunned by the sudden change of Peter's plans, but the bitterness she had felt was long gone, and only a soft sorrow remained. Peter wouldn't be here to help her through the coming months - but she had started work on her plans and had known already that he wouldn't be able to help her as he had always done previously. She settled into her sofa, opening the small notebook of calculations and actions she had brought back from her break, nodding her head as they made sense yet again. She was idly scrolling through news feeds on her phone, when it suddenly rang.

"Munro!" she answered. "Is everything okay? Thanks again for letting me stay at the cottage, it was amazing. Oh! Oh no..." she gasped.

Bev listened intently, letting Munro impart all his news before she reacted again. Lana's father had suffered a sudden heart attack, and the consultants reported that it had been very serious. He was in intensive care and may need surgery overnight. Lana and her mother were there, waiting for news. Both Munro and Jen were at their respective homes with their children, waiting for word.

"Oh Munro, I am so sorry to hear that," Bev replied. "Please tell Lana I'm thinking of them all and hoping for the best. He's in good hands there, at least." She paused once more, listening carefully through her shock and worry for her friends.

"Of course – no, of course I totally understand. They've all been through so much; family must come first. I couldn't ask Lana to deal with the committee or anything at this time, especially when I'm no longer involved. No, she needs to focus on what's important, her dad and family. I'll let them know, tell her she doesn't need to do anything. Do any of you need anything? I can be there first thing tomorrow if I can help at all?" she offered, looking at her wine glass in disgust and discarding it on the side table. She nodded as he declined her offer. "Okay. But please let me know if anything comes up that I can help with, anything at all. I'm just so sorry to hear this, Munro. Okay, all the best."

Munro ended the call, and Bev sat, stunned for the third time that evening, uncertain of what to do. She couldn't help, felt literally useless, knowing that her thoughts and prayers were all she could offer, and of no practical use. She quickly emailed the mental health committee organisers, letting them know that Lana's previous testimonies were as far as her friend was willing to go, that she needed to focus on her family from now. They would understand; Bev entirely understood. But that didn't ease the hollow hurt at her core, as she sat feeling so very alone in her home. She picked up her wineglass and took a large mouthful, despising herself for being so self-absorbed, but somehow unable to stop.

Chapter 27 – Friday 24th July

Lana stretched her back, surprised that the creaking and straining of her muscles didn't reverberate down the sparse beige corridor in which she sat. The linoleum beneath her feet was scored by the rubber of countless soles and wheels, and opposite her, the hatching of the reinforced glass window made the view out onto the concrete courtyard even more miserable. She grimaced, thinking over the hours she had spent here, lurking or pacing to pass the time until visitors were permitted into the ward. On that first night, the fear she had experienced had been overwhelming, but she had forced her body to be still, trying to share a false calm with her terrified mum. Since, she had become more accustomed to the surroundings, and as her dad had improved in recent days, the tension had been replaced with a feeling of hiatus, her life on hold as she sat impatiently. The dull décor of the corridor perfectly suited the ennui she felt now.

Her mind wandered, interrupted only by an elderly lady passing through the ward's double doors to her right, heading for the hospital concourse and its shops and cafes, heedless of the incongruity of her dressing gown and slippers. Lana slipped back into her mindless musings. Her mother was at home, waiting impatiently for Lana's return; she had already picked up the few groceries they had needed for their dinner, so that she could head straight home after this stop. She idly hoped the sun wouldn't come out and wilt the lettuce in the heat of the car.

The double doors clanged open once again, and Lana glanced up at a skinny, stooped old man being wheeled in a chair, his breathing laboured, his head down and hands shaky as they tried to grasp the walking stick in his lap. Her heart went out to him: wherever he was going, he would be exhausted after a few steps. She didn't let her glance linger, wary of invading his privacy as he struggled.

"Lana!" croaked a voice. "You just sitting there?"

She gaped up; shock tinged with horror chilling her as she realised her mistake. "Dad?" she managed. "I thought the nurse would have me come get you!"

"He's been ready for hours," the nurse behind the chair replied. "We were just waiting for his meds to come from the dispensary. As soon as they did, he insisted we get him home straight away," she smiled. "His things are here. You can bring your car around to the pick-up point - just leave the chair at the front door when you're finished with it," she advised.

Lana took command of the small overnight bag and the chair, grateful that her face would be hidden from her dad's view while she recovered from the shock. She had been horrified on the first visits, seeing how pale, tired, and suddenly aged her dad had seemed, just hours after his attack and the emergency surgery which had followed. But as he had recovered his colour, his humour and his breath, she had become accustomed to seeing him at rest, sitting up in bed in the ward, cheerfully chatting with the other patients. Seeing him so suddenly, in such a different light... Would her father now be as old and weak as he appeared? She was glad she had agreed to stay with her parents for a time, tackling the chores that neither parent could now manage.

By the time they were home, and welcomed by the rest of the family, Lana had recovered. Peter was ensconced in his rocking chair, Todd at his feet and reluctant to allow his master to leave him ever again. Stuart was playing happily outside with a putting practice set, and Robbie was showing his grandad his latest favourite toys. Munro followed Lana into the kitchen, carrying mugs to be refilled.

"How are you doing?" he asked softly as she filled the kettle.

Lana shook her head dismally. "I hadn't realised how weak he would be. I'm glad he's home, but I'm worried for him. It gave me a bit of a fright, seeing how hard he found it to get home."

Munro nodded. "He's been through a massive ordeal. They're happy with the results of his surgery, though, so now he's able to just focus on his rehabilitation. You'll be surprised how quickly he'll get his strength back, with fresh air and a gentle ramp up of walks."

Lana felt tears prickling at the back of her eyes. "I know that, really. I just keep catastrophising, you know? How would they manage, if he was like this for long? I feel like he's suddenly... Well, an old man. I've never thought of him that way before."

She busied herself by rinsing mugs and warming the

teapot, and Munro left her to collect herself, knowing that any advice would be something she already knew.

"I'm overreacting, I think," she eventually smiled with a shrug.

"Natural," rebutted Munro. "And he's not old. Soon, he'll be back as able as ever, I'm sure of it. Trust me, I'm a doctor," he quipped with a self-mocking tap on his nose.

They were interrupted by Jen bringing Robbie through the room. "Time for us to head home," she advised.

"Bath!" Robbie proudly proclaimed.

"Oh, you lucky little boy," Lana praised. "I might have a nice bath tonight, too. Can I borrow your duckies?" she joked.

But Robbie had said all he wanted, shyly tucking his smiling face into his mum's neck and clutching his toy to his chest.

Lana and Munro headed back out into the warm conservatory, where Lana's mum was sitting back with a smile as Peter stroked Todd's ears and shoulders contentedly.

"I feel better already, just for being home," he announced. "A proper night's sleep in my own bed ahead of me, homemade food, and all my favourite people here... And you, Todd. Such a good boy! I just need to get better and get back down to the b-e-a-c-h," he spelled out in a whisper. "Having a doctor in the family will come in handy for that!"

"Hah!" Lana interjected. "Don't say that - he's already been holding forth on how trustworthy his advice is," she laughed.

But Munro was more serious. "Taking it easy at first will be key. It's important to listen to your body, not tire yourself too much, and build up your strength. But I'm sure you'll be back on the... seaside soon!" he stopped himself in the nick of time.

Later, Lana walked Munro and Stuart home, enjoying the late summer evening. Stuart was thrilled to be up a little later than usual, enjoying the trust his dad had placed in him to go to bed as soon as they got home, and not be grumpy in the morning.

"I'm definitely getting to be bigger now," he advised them. "When I got up yesterday, I tiptoed downstairs and made myself breakfast, Lana!"

"Yes," his dad agreed. "And I'm so used to you waking me up that I slept in, and we were nearly both late!" he added, tousling Stuart's hair affectionately. "We'll need to start setting an alarm."

"Lana always sets an alarm," Stuart observed. "I hear it sometimes, but if it's too early I just stay in bed. When Lana comes to live with us, we can just use hers," he decided innocently.

Lana was surprised by the sudden segue but didn't let it show when she replied.

"For a while, I'll be staying with my dad to make sure he gets better. But after that I can come back to staying sometimes at the weekends when I won't be responsible for messing up your morning routines," she answered him with a soft laugh.

Stuart, however, looked puzzled by this answer. "But when you get married, you'll come and live with us, won't you?" he asked. "Dad? I just heard you..."

"Okay, okay!" Munro interjected, somehow sounding both exasperated and amused with his forthright son.

He had stopped beneath the trees which lined his driveway, and they stood starkly black against the backdrop of the cobalt evening sky. He turned to Lana, smiling ruefully.

"I wanted this to be a surprise, maybe plan a little something, but..." he shrugged expressively. "Lana, I spoke to your dad tonight while you were in the loo. I wanted his blessing, and he was happy to agree. Lana, will you marry me?" He dropped to one knee, then looked crestfallen. "I have a ring, but I don't have it with me," he rued.

Stuart was overjoyed, jumping on the spot and cheering as if his dad had scored a winning goal in the final minute of play. Lana's heart was thumping in her ribs, the goosebumps standing out across her bare skin highlighting her shock. She looked into Munro's hopeful face, and back at Stuart's more confident, happy one. Her first reaction was to list all the reasons why it would be... too soon, the wrong time, things had been so hectic... but then she realised that none of that was true. Nothing else was important, other than the people she had been with that evening. Life was too short for excuses and delays, too short for anything but love and happiness to be foremost.

"Yes!" she exclaimed, her grin belying the tears

streaming down her cheeks suddenly. "Yes, of course I'll marry you! If you're both sure you want me?" she suddenly worried.

But her concern was needless. Munro rose to embrace her - or kiss her – but she would never know which. Stuart suddenly sped into their space, throwing his arms around both their waists. Suddenly, they were all laughing and hugging and bouncing and saying "Yes, yes!" at the same time, and his excitement was everyone's.

It was after midnight by the time Lana returned to her parents' home, and while she was exhausted by the long day, she was unsure whether she could sleep. Once they had tucked Stuart into bed, Munro had disappeared into his study, returning with a ring box she could tell had been treasured for many years.

"This was my grandmother's," he advised soberly. "You don't need to use it if you don't want to," he stressed. "Ann didn't, she had dreamed of a particular style of ring for years. So, it's only your engagement ring if you like it," he had added, almost shyly.

Now, the stunning ring – a platinum band set with an Asscher-cut emerald flanked by diamonds beautiful enough to each be impressive solitaires - nestled in her jeans pocket. It had fitted perfectly, surprising them both, and she had worn it home, checking it every so often when she struggled to believe it had all truly happened. But she had removed it at the gate, so as not to spoil the surprise of her news. Now, she was curious to see a lamp still on in the lounge, and found her mum still awake, reading in her favourite chair by her bookcase.

"I thought you'd be asleep?" she asked softly, despite her dad being far down the hall.

Her mum smiled tiredly. "Oh, it's been such a long day, and you've had a hard time of it, running back and forward to do everything for us while you juggle your own life. You seemed out of sorts when you first got home, so I thought I'd wait up and check you were okay."

Lana's heart was touched again, and she wondered if she would be as good a parent as had blessed her own life. She smiled, thinking of Stuart's buoyant excitement at her being his step mum, and eventual dismay at being made to keep his promise to go to bed.

"I'm fine. It was a bit of a shock seeing Dad in the wheelchair," she admitted. "He looked so frail." Her mum nodded her understanding. "But it's good to see him home and happy now."

"He's happy when you and Jen are both happy," her mum reminded her. "You girls are his life. He'll follow doctor's orders, believe me – he'll do anything to make sure he's here with you both for as long as he possibly can be. We both will; I hope you know that," she concluded, taking Lana's hand in her own.

"I do," Lana agreed. "And let's hope that's for a long, long time yet. No more scares like this!" she pleaded to an unnamed power.

"Indeed," her mum seconded. "Only happy surprises from now on, please!"

Lana watched her mum carefully, knowing Munro had told them he would be proposing sometime soon, once he'd had time to plan. Did her mum suspect? Was she fishing for news, or just idly joking? She decided that the difference was entirely irrelevant: she couldn't keep her excitement to herself any longer.

"Actually, Mum... I do have some news," she braved, reaching into her pocket.

Chapter 28 – Saturday 25th July

Bev ushered the earnest young man through her front door, grateful to close it behind him and breathe freely again. He had been impeccably dressed in a business suit and highly polished shoes, but his aftershave had been excessive and overpowering. She rushed to her windows to air out her space.

As she pottered in the kitchen, enjoying the ritual of brewing her coffee, she smiled to herself. Her visitor's news had been good, and soon she would be able to stop taking Munro's money to ensure she could make ends meet. She checked her to-do list; in a few days she would return her unnecessarily large car, and that would be the last of her immediate financial concerns. Today and tomorrow, she would declutter and sort everything she owned, and run carloads to the charity shops and recycling facilities while she had the large boot space to hand. She sipped her coffee contentedly, feeling that – at last – she was doing something productive.

She had tried to relax, tried to pivot, tried to re-imagine herself and her life – but she just could not bring herself to walk away from what she saw as a pending disaster. In her heart, she knew that her work was going to be used to ruin lives, rather than improve them – and she could not rest until she had stopped that from being possible. Peter, Munro, and her former colleagues would say she was being overly paranoid, worrying about a future that may not come to pass, taking personal responsibility for decisions made way beyond her realm of influence. But she now knew that many others worried as she did - and had good evidence to support their concerns. Martha and Chris had both thoroughly approved of her decision to try and continue campaigning, agreeing that only Bev could decide what her conscience would allow. She was keeping them up to date with her progress, and they had become her closest allies now that Lana and Munro had stepped back from their commitments and Peter had become absorbed in planning his big move.

She felt her spirits dip, knowing that she didn't grudge her friends their lives, their happiness, or their optimism, but somehow unable to stop feeling alone, even abandoned. When Munro had called her at breakfast, and told her of his engagement, she was overjoyed for her two friends and touched that she had been his first port of call with the good news. But once they had said their goodbyes, she had been left feeling flat: somehow, this cemented the differences between them. Munro and Lana were moving on with their lives, continuing the paths they had individually forged, but now walking them together. Bev's path had ended, and now she had chosen a new one, one which took her away from those she was closest to. She hadn't seen much of her family for years, now – decades, she realised – and her work, and her closeness to Peter had become the core pillars of her life. She hadn't had successful relationships, or exciting holidays, a hobby, or even many friends for such a long time, now. She resolved to make more effort in future, to spend her time with those who shared her beliefs and passions.

That could all begin in just a week or two, she realised with a start.

She spun slowly in the centre of her lounge, mentally cataloguing her possessions, and pondering which would be useful in future, which she would cherish for years to come, and which would be taking a trip in her car this weekend. She felt her resolve stiffen, knowing that it would be best to carry as little physical baggage as emotional. With a firm nod, she started to open drawers and cupboards, and unearthed her stash of cardboard boxes and bubble wrap.

Later, she slumped into her sofa, her knees and ankles aching, but her heart lighter. An entire wall of her hall was filled with stacks of boxes, each one scribbled with their destination. She sipped the too-hot tea she had just made, then checked another task off her list; she had achieved more than she expected today. She smiled at the brochure lying beside her list, on which a bland grey van was parked amongst stunning views, tinted windows giving little hint of the pristine living space within it. She had reserved the same model just the previous weekend, using what remained of her savings as a deposit. The deal she had just agreed this morning would cover the remaining payment and leave her with a decent sum for her future; her home had been a wise investment, it appeared.

She decided to treat herself to indulgences while she could, so she ordered some over-priced takeaway food to be delivered and selected her favourite movie on the massive television she had rarely watched. She visited her beautiful but now sparsely populated kitchen, grabbing cutlery and crockery, and made herself a tall glass of perfectly balanced gin and tonic, with a squeeze and slice of lime and a scattering of fresh mint leaves. She would make the most of her space and luxuries while they were still hers.

Chapter 29 – Sunday 30th August

Lana had woken early, as she often did in Munro's bedroom. The sun was bright where the curtains didn't quite meet, and she lay comfortably, watching Munro sleep while she appreciated this quiet moment to herself. The dim, fractured light cast dark shadows under his eyes, making him look more drawn and tired than he truly was. She smiled: somehow despite this he was still her handsome Munro, still as attractive as ever. Last night, they had celebrated their engagement, and Lind had held forth in a spontaneous speech, berating Lana for stealing the town's most coveted bachelor. Sanj had folded his arms in mock anger at this, and Lind had tactfully added that Munro hadn't been to their taste, this being the only reason he was available for Lana to pinch. Lana and Munro's families had been there, too, and Lana was pleased to see Munro's parents accepting their friends and her family equally well. His mother had quietly hugged Lana, telling her how lovely it was to see her mum's ring looking so beautiful on her hand. Laurie, and many of the practice partners and staff had also come along, and the party, held in a private room in one of the local bars, had been a great – if tiring – success. Her father had looked stronger and happier than he had done since his hospitalisation, and Lana had finally stopped hovering over him when he pointedly told her that she was cramping his style. Late in the evening, Lana had looked from her friends to her family, and felt a rush of emotion she didn't succeed at hiding.

"Hey," Munro had chided her. "Happy occasion!" He had winked.

Lana had smiled, stepping under his shoulder and wrapping his arm around her. "It's all a bit too perfect," she had explained. "Although, I wish Bev and Pete could have made it. Have you heard back from her yet?"

"No," Munro had frowned lightly, "and neither has Pete. I'll chase her next week."

Now, Lana recreated that moment, shifting Munro's arm and rummaging until she was resting her head on his shoulder, wrapping him around her and her around him. He stirred and woke with a relaxed smile.

"Are you really awake, already?" he mumbled. "We were up 'til two... Thank God for Laurie bringing Stuart home at a decent time, your friends are animals," he complained, rubbing his forehead and leaning into her.

"I didn't make you drink all that single malt with your dad and Dr Clegg," Lana rebutted. "Don't blame me or my friends." She handed him a glass of water, gently.

"Thanks," he muttered as he sipped. "I'm glad we don't have much to do today. Although I do think we need to start planning a certain wedding: I can't remember a single person who didn't complain that we weren't getting organised," he recalled.

"Mhmm," Lana agreed. "I've been thinking about that. How would you feel about doing it here, in the house or the garden? We don't want lots of people – in fact, there wouldn't be many more than last night. We could get caterers in, so it wouldn't be too much work. It would be more private here, and less stressful, and it's close to home for so many people. Your mum and dad could just stay here," she concluded.

"That's not a bad idea," Munro agreed, surprised. "I wondered if you might change your mind about a church, or the beach, or something? Or might want a bigger fuss?"

"God, no," Lana laughed. "As little fuss as possible, please! We could have it pretty much when we wanted, too, instead of needing to book a hotel, years in advance."

"Do weddings not take years to organise, anyway?" Munro countered, playing devil's advocate.

"Nah," Lana disagreed. "A caterer, a florist, a registrar, some outfits. I really don't want to make it too complicated." She paused for thought, checking Munro was paying attention before she continued. "I'm not sure I want to leave it too long, to be honest. I know it sounds daft, and I know my dad is fine now, but... Well, what happened gave me a fright. He's always talked about walking me down the aisle - getting married wouldn't feel the same without everyone there, and..."

Munro interrupted her. "It doesn't sound daft at all. You've all had a scare - and whether your worries are founded or not, if it makes you feel better to get married sooner rather than later? Well, that's what we'll do. How long would we need to get things arranged?"

Lana shrugged. "A few months? I know the registrars need notice, and we'd need to decide on food and things. But that's at least October, and the weather wouldn't be great by then," she mused.

"So what?" Munro laughed. "We have a big house with big rooms we hardly use. We can set up the big back room for the ceremony, have the food and drinks in the kitchen and the dining room, and people can mingle wherever they like. We could do it at any time of year. How about Christmas or New Year? Everyone gets together then, anyway, and the house is always decorated."

Lana felt a stir of excitement, and saw it mirrored in Munro's eyes. They had the start of a plan, and as they talked it over, and added embellishments to make the occasion theirs instead of sticking to traditions, she knew they were on the right path. She watched Munro as he carefully compared the benefits of the two times, before deciding that Christmas Eve would be perfect, so long as the registrars would agree. "And enough locums owe me a favour that they'll agree to cover my leave even over the holiday season," he concluded, his eyes gleaming as he planned. "Which would you prefer for a honeymoon: a tropical beach or a ski resort?" he laughed.

Lana couldn't resist his infectious enthusiasm, and she fell back into his arms, giggling.

"Whatever doctor thinks is best," she teased, before they celebrated their decision in the best way she could possibly imagine.

That morning, as they were all in the kitchen finishing

off a late breakfast, the doorbell rang. Laurie pushed back her chair before they could rise.

"Let me get it, you two relax. I've got to head home shortly, anyway, and you both look like you could use a second tea from the pot!" she joked.

They heard her open the door, but both were surprised when she led Peter Bryant into the room.

"Pete!" Munro exclaimed. "I thought you were in Canada this weekend; you missed the party last night. Is everything okay?" He rapidly changed tack as he registered the seriousness of his friend's expression.

"I'm a bit worried about Bev, to be honest," he started to explain, as Laurie tempted Stuart into another room to build some Lego. "Have you heard anything back from her since we last spoke?" he checked.

"No," Munro replied, setting coffee to brew. "I've messaged her a few times this week – she hasn't replied. Is she not at home?"

"No, that's the thing that has me worried. I was meant to be heading out to Ottawa on Friday night," he started to explain. "But before I left the clinic, the police stopped by, asking if I'd seen her. I explained I hadn't, but they wouldn't tell me why they were looking for her – just advised that I must call them as soon as possible if I heard from her. I went to her flat - and someone else is living there! She's sold it; it finalised last week. It was all agreed in July, apparently - they did all their dealings through a solicitor. I called her parents, but they haven't heard from her, either – and they've had the police call in as well! I don't know what's going on, Munro, it's all so bizarre," he concluded.

"Her solicitor must have a way of contacting her, though. Did you find who it was?" Munro asked.

"The woman said it was all through one of the big conveyancing firms, so she didn't use her usual guy. I could give him a call, but I'm not sure he would help, even if he does know anything," Pete worried.

"She must be living somewhere, though," Lana interrupted. "What about all her things, her car? I have no idea how to find someone other than going to the police, and they're already looking for her. What do you think she's done?"

"I honestly don't know," Peter admitted. "She went a bit quiet after I told her I'd be taking the job in Ottawa; I thought she just needed some space. I've been so busy: wrapping up our work here, arranging to let my house, packing everything away... I had no idea she might be doing the same thing! I feel terrible, she must have felt so alone these last few weeks."

Lana could see how deeply worried he was, and the guilt which was already gnawing at him.

"Don't blame yourself too much," she advised. "Bev must have decided to keep this secret, for whatever reason – you've both been in touch with her, and she gave no clue to what she's been planning and organising. What could she have done?"

But Peter shook his head dismally. "I have no idea. I've even tried asking if Martha or Chris have heard from her, but both the numbers I had for them have been disconnected."

They talked for over an hour, trying to come up with a way to find out more, but emerged defeated.

"We can only tell all this to the police, explain how concerned we are," Munro repeated. "Whatever reason they're looking for her, at least then she'll be recorded as a missing person."

Peter nodded. "What should I do, Munro? I'm due to fly out to Ottawa to start work in just two weeks. I can't leave without knowing she's okay."

But Munro contradicted him. "No. No, you must go. Whatever has happened, Bev wouldn't want you to squander this opportunity. There's nothing much you could do here, and between us and Bev's family there will be plenty people to push for answers. Keep trying to contact her, let her know what you're doing – but go on with your plans. We're just a flight away, once she gets in touch and we know what's going on."

Lana took over from Laurie, distracting Stuart as the police arrived and Munro and Peter explained their concerns. They called Bev's parents again while the police were there, giving them contact details of the officers who had already been in touch. By mid-afternoon, they all realised how futile their efforts were.

"It does look very much like Bev planned to disappear off the radar for a while," Peter finally admitted. "We can only hope she's at a beach resort someplace enjoying life and getting over all this – and that she'll get back in touch soon. I hope she knows how important she is," he added as he prepared to leave.

"We'll stay in touch; I'm sure it will all be clear and

sorted soon," Munro replied, with a conviction Lana wasn't sure he felt.

Chapter 30 – Thursday December 24th, Christmas Eve

Lana stood at the window of her childhood bedroom, looking out at a view she had known since her earliest memories, changed only by maturing greenery. Downstairs, she could hear her mum and Jen chattering and teasing each other as they got ready to leave the house. She looked at her phone yet again, hoping beyond hope that she would have a message, an explanation, anything which would grant Munro some extra peace of mind before they wed. But no. Bev was still maintaining the silence that had fallen the previous summer. Nothing had come of the police investigations, and they had never been informed as to why the force wanted to speak to her themselves. One day in October, Lana had found an image on a news site, of a civil rights protest in London, and had wondered at the hooded figure standing beside Martha at the forefront, comparing their heights and builds and struggling to decide whether there was a chance it could be her friend. But in the end, this further minor mystery didn't help settle the anxiety they all felt when they thought of the brilliant clinician and kind woman they missed so deeply. Munro had known of her hope that Bev would get in touch before they married, but he himself felt less optimistic.

"Bev will absolutely wish us the best – assuming she knows – but whatever she's doing, she's completely committed to it. Otherwise, we'd have heard from her by now," he had advised. "It's fine. We'll miss her, but we won't let that spoil our day."

Lana's reverie was broken by her sister bursting into the room.

"Mum and I are away up there. Are you sure you want to walk?" she checked yet again.

"Yes!" Lana laughed. "It's hardly any distance, and I want some time with Dad. Plus, we don't want a gazillion cars in the driveway to move tomorrow," she laughed. "Do I look fine?" she worried, suddenly.

"You look amazing," Jen reassured her. "That word gets used too often, I admit - but it's still the best one for how you look right now. We'll see you there, then. Don't leave too soon: Dad'll frogmarch you there and you'll be early. I can't believe how fitness-obsessed he is now!" She left with a fond roll of her eyes and a big smile.

Lana's father came in through the door as she left. "Oh, Lana," he breathed. "My lovely girl. Are we allowed a hug, or do you crumple?"

Lana laughed. "Oh, hugging is fine," she replied, grabbing him for a tight squeeze. "But crumpling isn't the problem, it's getting scratched by sequins! I may have gone slightly overboard."

She looked back into her full-length mirror, checking for flaws. Her dress was an art-deco throwback: cape sleeves and a modest neckline, gathered tightly about her waistline, then flowing freely into a small train. It was a brilliant white, with myriad beads and sequins giving the appearance of fan shapes and sleek lines. At this stage, anything she might tinker with would take too long and make too little difference, so she squared her shoulders, grinned, and shrugged her way into a glorious white fake fur jacket she had borrowed from Lind, then led her father down the stairs.

They checked the doors one last time, then settled Todd into his basket for the evening before leaving the house. Lana was surprised to see their neighbours and some of her parents' friends clustered around the front gate, lit by streetlights and wrapped up against the cold, tears in more than one set of eyes. She realised that she had known these people her whole life, been gently encouraged and praised by them for her achievements, been watched with fondness from a polite distance, but no less loved for that.

"Oh, don't!" she pleaded. "Don't set me off crying, I was so careful with my makeup," she laughed.

More hugs and good wishes later, she headed off uphill, holding her father's hand gratefully, glad of his solid and reassuring presence while she processed the tumult of emotions she felt.

"I thought I was all organised," she explained. "Everything was ready, so I wouldn't be nervous, or a teary wreck. But it all suddenly seems quite a big deal."

Peter squeezed her hand gently, maintaining the gentle pace they had set.

"That's okay. It is a big deal; it's a big day. It's a big commitment you're about to make, and – hopefully! - an incredibly happy day for you both. It's normal to feel a bit overwhelmed. If you need a minute, or need to talk, just say," he offered.

"No, I'm fine really. No doubts or anything. I just didn't expect to be so... raw. So affected by everyone coming to see us. God knows what I'll be like when I see everyone at the ceremony. What if I make a berk of myself, Dad?" she asked, surprised at how vulnerable she felt.

"What kind of berk?" Peter smartly probed.

"I might cry, or get the shakes... My hands aren't steady even now!"

Peter stopped, turning his daughter to face him. "Then they'll know how important this is to you. They'll understand how much this means to you. They'll love you for it, not think you're a berk." He kissed her gently on the forehead, something he had done every night when she was a child. They each took a breath, then moved on.

As they entered Munro's tree-lined drive, they were surprised at how quiet the house seemed from the outside. A few extra cars, the Christmas lights twinkling, but otherwise not so different from the previous evening, when Lana had left the house as a single woman for the last time.

"Everyone will be in the big back room," she reminded them both. "We've set up an aisle and everything," she chuckled. "That room barely gets used, usually. Now, it won't ever feel the same!"

"Come on, then," he replied. "Let's not leave the poor boy on tenterhooks. Let's get you up that aisle."

They snuck in the front door, Lana feeling curiously nervous while entering a house she knew so well. The hall was magnificent, the massive side table dominated by a spectacular Christmas floral arrangement, and the eye drawn down the hall by their traditionally decorated tree. The rooms to either side were empty, no one lurking in the family lounge or Stuart's playroom. Passing the tree, they glanced into the formal dining room, and Lana beamed to see the table she had fastidiously set the previous evening, now looking even better with the addition of the elegant floral centrepieces she had ordered. The glass door to the spacious kitchen dining revealed the caterers and their mouth-watering buffet, and Lana grinned back when they both waved and gave her a thumbs-up. That left only two doors, one to the downstairs loo, and one into Munro's large but usually sparsely furnished library and study. For today, they had moved all the furniture out to the garage, leaving only the shelves which lined three of the walls, a pair of small side tables in front of the bay window to hold flowers, some candelabras, and the rows of borrowed dining chairs they had set up for their guests.

Lana looked to her dad, realising that now, suddenly, her nerves had settled, and she was ready to take this next step. She didn't trust herself to speak, simply tilting her head towards the door with a smile.

They entered together, arm in arm, and Lana's stomach flipped when she saw Munro waiting for her at the window. Stuart was at his side, unable to be a legal witness, but there to play every other part of the best man's role. Munro first looked serious, nervous, perhaps even a little dumb founded, but then slowly broke into the happiest of smiles, before he and Stuart welcomed her with their identical grins. Their registrar nodded encouragingly as Lana joined them, and her father sat down beside her mum and the rest of their family and friends. Finally, Lana broke Munro's gaze to look across at their guests, feeling a well of gratitude and amazement as she took in the effort they had made with their outfits, and the happiness they all expressed.

The registrar had sent them a transcript of their brief introduction, reading and vows - but even so, Lana was unprepared for how well she encompassed everyone into the spirit of the ceremony, somehow tempering the seriousness of their commitment with a shared joy. Every so often, she glanced into Munro's eyes, and he squeezed her hand where he had automatically held it. Suddenly, it was time for them to repeat their vows, and she locked eyes with this man she loved, looking away only when it was time for Stuart to produce the rings which they each spoke of.

"Following these binding declarations, which you have made before me and in the presence of your witnesses, it is now my honour to pronounce you, Munro and you Lana, to be husband and wife," the registrar concluded, and suddenly they were bound together. As they signed paperwork, and posed for photos, making sure Stuart didn't get separated from them in the swarm of good wishes, they both grinned. This was exactly what they had hoped for.

The cake was cut, champagne was poured, and the playlist Munro and Lana had carefully curated was playing gently throughout the house. The buffet food was superb, and their guests were spread through the rooms, enjoying each other's company as much as the food. They had planned no speeches, or traditional trappings of a wedding reception, but Lind was holding court in the kitchen, telling bright stories of their exploits, making everyone laugh. Lana stuck to Munro like glue, conflicted between wanting to speak to all their guests but not wanting to leave his side for a moment. Everyone understood.

Her father approached, looking slightly tipsy. "So - what's the plan for tomorrow? What time are you all coming over?"

Lana glanced across the room, to where Stuart was happily showing Laurie the photos he had taken so far. She risked replying, quietly.

"Sometime late morning, I suspect. We're not sure when he'll wake, if he's up later tonight - but I'll ping you once we're up, so you've got a bit of warning. We're still a bit worried that he'll feel left out if he knows we're going away on Saturday, so we're waiting to pack after we've left him at yours. With it just being a couple of nights, and you taking him to Crieff, he'll probably never know."

The family were all spending Christmas Day together, then on Boxing Day Lana's parents had offered to take Stuart with them, Jen and Robbie for a stay at a nearby hotel, which specialised in activities for families of all ages, but still catered for the adults with great restaurants, bars and a spa. Stuart had jumped at the chance, and Munro had been touched by how confident he had been, and how comfortable he already was with his new grandparents and auntie. But neither he nor Lana had felt it was fair to tell him they were going on a trip without him, a honeymoon that didn't include children, a country hotel of their own. They'd chickened out up to now.

They agreed the plan for the next day, and Peter moved on, leaving Lana and Munro briefly alone by the buffet.

"Well, Mrs Alexander. How does it feel?" he smiled.

Lana surprised herself by pausing to take the question seriously. "I'm happy – so happy. But I didn't expect to feel any different, and I do. It's weird. A good weird," she giggled at his alarmed expression. "I don't know if it was just what the registrar said, or just having everyone here together - or maybe just the fizz," she laughed again, "but... I do feel like we're one big family now. That you and I are not just married, but part of something much larger. It's lovely."

Munro's eyes were shining. "Yes," he managed, before kissing her intensely.

"Enough of that! Plenty time for that after your guests have left," laughed Munro's mum. "I'd like to borrow my namesake Mrs Alexander, if it's alright with you." She didn't wait for Munro's approval, dragging Lana out of his reach and into the lounge, where she settled them both into the sofa.

"We wanted to give you something. Not your wedding gift – Munro already has that, and will explain later," she added intriguingly. "But something just for you, to welcome you to our little family." She sobered slightly, before continuing. "You've made such a difference to Munro - and Stuart – and we appreciate it so much. I don't know if you realise how... meagre his life was, after Ann died. He was so lost. He had Stuart, and kept up appearances for him, and eventually they seemed happy whenever we saw them together. But... well, we could see it. As soon as Stuart left the room, or went to bed, he... deflated. Stuart was all he had to keep him going. Now - this last year or so – he's so much happier, but also so much more alive. We have our son back, and that's down to you. So, anyway - we want you to have this. It's just a little thing, but we wanted you to wear it and remember how much you mean to us both, even if we are a little reserved and fuddy-duddy," she laughed.

Lana was touched, but unsure what to say. "I..." she

faltered.

"No, no, you don't have to say anything. And don't take it as pressure, please. It's not up to you to keep him happy forever. It's just that we're grateful, and we want you to know."

Lana nodded, tears brimming yet again. She shook them off, then opened the small parcel she had been handed. The gift paper opened in fragile petals, eventually revealing a deep burgundy velvet box, hinged along its longest side, which just fitted in her palm. She fought against the tiny but strong hinges, and gasped as it opened. Nestled in more deep red velvet was a stunning gold charm bracelet, delicate yet strong. On it were a number of dainty charms, including a small gold chapel, an engraved bible, a pair of engagement and wedding rings, a love heart, and a cluster of clasped hands.

"This is beautiful," she breathed.

"It was given to my mother, when she wed. The same woman who handed down that ring," she smiled, nodding to Lana's wedding finger, now graced with both the exquisite engagement ring and a matching plain platinum band. "It might be too old-fashioned for you to wear," she started to worry.

"No!" Lana interjected. "It's perfect. The charms are so detailed!" she added as she realised that the church opened up to reveal a miniature wedding couple kneeling before an altar, and the bible contained folded paper pages with the Lord's Prayer printed in miniscule font. "Thank you so much. Are you sure?"

No more words were needed from her, as her mother-in-law pulled her into her embrace. "It's all yours, my dear," she heard, whispered into her ear.

"Lana! Lana!" Stuart burst into the room. "I've just been hearing about honeymoons!" he explained. "You and Dad need one!"

Lana was startled, and Munro had stepped into the doorway, looking a little concerned - but she accepted that she shouldn't be surprised. Stuart was too smart to keep secrets from.

"Well..." she tailed off, as he talked over her.

"You need to go away! You should have gone away tonight, in fact! You're doing it all wrong!" he added.

"No, we are not!" Lana corrected him, quickly. "We're special. We're not just a newly married couple - we're a new family. We're spending our first night here, as a family, the way we'll spend all the rest of our nights. I think that's spot on," she explained.

"Oh," said Stuart, re-thinking. "But when do you get a holiday, then?" he asked, determined not to let the issue slide.

"Actually," his dad intervened, ruffling his hair in a gesture already so familiar to Lana. "I have some surprises. One for Lana, and one for you both."

Lana was startled at this news, but saw that Munro's parents were sharing a grin, and remembered Munro quickly ending a few phone calls in the last few weeks.

"What have you been up to?" she demanded, jokingly.

"Stuart, I have to confess," he started. "I'm taking Lana away to a posh hotel while you're away on holiday." Stuart grinned happily, proving that Lana still worried too much about his feelings being more fragile than they truly were. "Lana, I also have a surprise for both of you," he continued. "In April, when the schools are off for Easter break, instead of going down to the cottage for a few days, we'll be going to Africa. To Namibia, to stay on a wildlife reserve – we can take tours to see all the big wildlife and have days just relaxing at the pool. Mum and Dad have arranged it all," he explained.

"Really?" Lana gasped. "That will be amazing! I've always wanted to go to Africa and see the wildlife, but it's so expensive and I'm never sure how much money really goes to the local people," she clarified.

"That's all taken care of," Munro's father spoke up. "It's a fantastic local enterprise, but still luxurious enough to be a real treat. Don't worry about a thing."

"Will I see an elephant?" Stuart suddenly realised.

"Yep," his dad grinned. "And giraffes, antelopes, leopards, rhinos... all sorts!"

Stuart threw himself into Lana's lap, as she gazed up at Munro in amazement.

"Best day ever!" he announced.

The party lasted late into the evening, but Lana was pleased when people started to drift off home before midnight, leaving only those dearest to her as the hall clock struck twelve, and they welcomed their first Christmas as a family.

"Merry Christmas, Stuart!" Lana wheezed, as he squished her ribs in a tight embrace.

"But off to bed! Santa will be doing his rounds: we all need to be asleep pronto!" Munro added.

As they tidied away the last few leftovers, turned off lights, locked their doors and windows, and headed to bed, Lana abruptly realised that this was now her life. This was her home, now, too. She put down the glasses she was carrying and took a breath.

"You okay?" Munro checked.

"God, yes," she reassured him. "Just realising how lucky I am, how happy I am. I love you," she told him for the hundredth time that evening.

"I love you, too," he replied. "Leave those and come to bed. We need to get you out of that dress, and it looks complicated," he grinned, with a comedic waggle of his eyebrows.

Outside, in the darkness of Munro's mature back gardens, a quiet figure wiped the tears from her cheeks. The un-draped windows had been a godsend, as had the easy access through a neighbour's unlocked gate and over the dividing stone wall. Even with the bright lights indoors, she had been cautious, skulking behind a large rhododendron and keeping far from the sensors of the security lights. She may not have heard their vows, but she had seen their faces, and the happiness there. She had watched them wed, and that was the best she could hope for. She wouldn't jeopardise their futures by associating with them, not when she knew that what she had planned was questionably moral, and definitely illegal. She wouldn't worry them by refusing to answer their questions, either.

"I wish you all the luck in the world," she whispered, tears catching in her voice. "You'll be so happy now; I'm so happy for you both. Let me worry about everything else. I'd do it all a thousand times over, for you all."

She turned, slunk through the shrubs and trees, and hopped back over the wall and into the dark.

Chapter 31 – Thursday 31st December

Bev settled into the beachfront bench, pulling her scarf tighter and appreciating the concrete and glass shelter which provided a windbreak on three sides as well as protection from the persistent chill drizzle. Here on the south coast, the winter days weren't as bitterly cold as they were in Edinburgh, but she had learned to be wary of the draining south-westerlies which dominated the weather from October to February. She pulled on her gloves, settled back into the badly designed seat, and picked up the insulated mug in which she had brought fresh coffee from her van. She was early, but believed it looked less pre-arranged if she was here well in advance of Martha. Two middle-aged women sharing a few moments of their morning would cause no comment.

She looked down the seafront, towards the vast white modernist arts centre which dominated the view, but she saw no one. In this, mostly elderly community, early morning walkers were rare until more clement weather arrived. A lone cyclist whizzed past from her left, enjoying the turn of speed they had gained as they descended from the cliffside path which broke up the uniformity of the coastal walk. Behind her, boxy blocks of flats remained in darkness, and she wondered where the cyclist was headed, bundled up in their layers. Perhaps an early start for work in one of the shops or cafes, she mused, given that all the schools and many businesses were shut for the holidays. She turned back towards the pavilion, and spotted a lone figure ambling along the esplanade, appearing entirely at ease with the weather conditions. She smiled, knowing the lie in that.

"Gods, but this is hideous. Give me proper rain any day; this "more than mist, less than rain, feel silly with a hood up but get wet otherwise" weather is just depressing," grumped Martha as she sat down primly at the far end of the bench. "No one will see us: can we not go into your van, where's there's heating?" she pleaded.

"You never know what an ancient insomniac might see from those windows," Bev gestured towards the flats. "We're still traceable by so much," she rued. "I'd rather disappear off the grid entirely, but that's just not possible these days if we want to drive, or travel, or hold a bank account. No. If anyone decided to investigate either of us, I'd rather they didn't automatically suspect the other just because we're a bit chilly. Have some not-sausage butty," she offered, unwrapping a towel and foil wrapped package of vegan sausage on fresh morning rolls. "Brown sauce," she advised.

They tucked into their modest breakfast, grateful for the relative privacy of the solid concrete behind which they sat.

"I feel like a twit, too," Bev admitted. "Like a wannabe Russian spy in a 1960s novel," she sighed. "We'd better be quick. Is everything on track? Any concerns?"

"No," Martha shook her head, speaking with her

mouth full. "Every detail you got for us has been proven correct; everything is in place. Don't worry. Stage one will start fifteen minutes before midnight, as agreed. Tomorrow is trickier to coordinate, due to the numbers of people involved... But we've heard from every one of your contacts, and they all say they'll be able to act at the right time; they're confident of success. Part three is automated and pre-scheduled, as you know. It should require no human intervention – which I still can't believe, it's so clever – and after that, our message will be out there, clear as day. I just hope we have enough undeniable evidence to sway opinion," she worried.

"If it isn't, then we'll find more. This is a marathon, not a sprint, Martha. We're in this for the long haul; not just for two days," Bev reiterated. "That's why it's so important we keep ourselves free from any suspicion, that nobody tries to take the limelight. I suspect we'll have a lot to do, over a long time. But we'll get there, whatever the cost," she added, with a cold certainty that she could tell surprised Martha.

"You've changed," the other woman confirmed. "You're harder; you're spending too much time with some of those hothead friends of Chris'. Don't let them make you less yourself, Bev. Remember you're a good person, and why you care so much" she advised, gently.

"I'm fine, honestly. None of this will hurt anyone, but it will affect many and it can't be covered up. We need to make an impact to ensure our voice is heard. It's the only way," Bev countered. "I'm still very much me," she laughed. "We should go. I'll send the next meeting details the usual way," she concluded, before gathering her mug and detritus, and heading back up over the short cliffside walk to the carpark where she had stopped just an hour before.

As she reached her van, she was glad to see that the streets were still quiet: no new cars had arrived, no parked cars had been driven away. Ideally, no one would know she had been here. She smiled, realising that she had taken to automatically keeping a low profile; it would stand her in good stead in the days to come. She tidied away her mug and the dishes she had used to prepare their breakfast and slid into the driver's seat. Her official excuse for being in the area was as a birdwatcher, so she headed to a nearby reedbed conservation area, and parked up before locking herself in, and bundling into her small bed for a nap; she'd had little sleep, and it would be a long day. She could rest before taking her binoculars to the small hide at dusk.

She woke to the sound of voices nearby, but casually took her time re-orienting herself before she climbed out of her bed and opened her blinds. Dog-walkers were bundling muddy-pawed hounds into the boot of their car, kicking clods of red clay turf from their boots before driving back towards the town. Bev relaxed with a cup of tea, then prepared herself for an hour or so outdoors. While her travels were mostly a series of pretences, she found she enjoyed the quiet solitude of her new life, and a little time enjoying a peaceful hobby was no burden. It allowed her time to think, to process everything she was orchestrating with her collaborators. She could introspect, ensuring she was still happy with the balance of her conscience, occasionally harking back to a religious belief she no longer held.

When darkness had once again fallen, she drove to her next overnight stop, taking the time to empty and refill her onboard tanks, as well as picking up fresh supplies and a few treats for the coming nights of celebrations. As she ensured her van was level, enjoying the feeling of being settled for the next few days, she realised that she was unexpectedly cheerful: her worries were temporarily allayed, and she was looking forward to a nice meal out. She undressed and showered, carefully dressed in the one nice outfit she had brought with her, then headed out.

"How was your meal?" the proprietor asked, collecting Bev's dinner plate from her small table by the open fire.

"It was fantastic," Bev replied honestly. "When you're away in a campervan, it's amazing how much you appreciate a meal that's been cooked in more than one pot," she laughed.

"Where's that accent from? Are you Scottish? I used to know a girl from Aberdeen, no idea what she was saying half the time. Do you celebrate the Hog thingy up there?" the woman quizzed her in a friendly fashion, leaning on one hip and smiling apologetically.

Bev grinned, appreciating the forthright company. "Hogmanay? We used to, when I was younger. Drinks and food with family and neighbours, people walking from house to house, visiting everyone, a real party atmosphere. But nowadays it's not really that different from your New Year's Eve celebrations here, and I'm a bit old for street parties or late nights, now," she grinned. "And the days of visiting your neighbours to first foot have kind of died out. It's a shame," she admitted.

"Well, you're welcome to stay here," the woman offered. "We're not fully booked or anything. There's a local folk band on from 9:30, but they're not too noisy. Bill does a wee Quiz of the Year at 10:30. Bar's open until 12:30, and we'll see in the bells with some sandwiches and stuff. Folk'll chat away to you no bother; it's a good night and we often have new faces."

Bev was intrigued, and despite knowing that she should keep to herself, she also knew she was desperate to sit amongst cheerful company. She found herself delaying her exit: first lingering over dessert, then coffee, then more drinks. By the time she was pulled into another table's quiz team, she no longer cared about any risk of being remembered, barely thinking about everything she had planned. She was enjoying herself, and distracting herself, and that was okay.

As the band headed back to their positions, she was in the middle of a debate about the current government, and whether their corruption was worse than their previous tenures, or whether it was simply more widely publicised in the modern age. She was listening to an elderly quiz teammate wax lyrical about the moral fibre of politicians in his youth, when there was a sudden ruckus about the bar, and the band's music petered out. The volume on the television was raised, and a news anchor confirmed what everyone hadn't quite believed they were seeing.

"We've had a massive power cut here on the Thames," he said. "We've lost all lighting, and only battery-powered devices are working. The celebrations are in turmoil, and revellers are confused and alarmed. I'm... I'm just hearing that there have also been power cuts in both Edinburgh and Cardiff, centred on their own festivities. Police are now asking the public to remain calm but disperse from the area. We don't know what has caused the power cuts, or what else might happen next, but we're being asked to leave..."

Bev was briefly as stunned as everyone else in the small, friendly, country pub, where cities and power cuts seemed so incongruous. But then she realised that this was exactly what she been waiting for: it had begun.

Chapter 32 – Saturday 2nd January

Lana rolled over in the large bed, squinting to check how light the day was behind the curtains. Munro shifted beside her, but she could see from the relaxed lines of his face that he wasn't quite awake just yet. She rolled back towards her bedside cabinet, relieved to see the large water glass there was mostly full.

"Ooft, I am so dehydrated," she complained under her breath. "Two days in a row of rich food and good wine, and I'm scuppered," she admitted.

"Uh-huh?" Munro hadn't yet opened his eyes, but his voice held a hint of amusement amongst the rusty creak of sleep-tightened vocal cords.

"Don't sound like that, I thought I did quite well to stop Dad plying me with all the red he fancied drinking himself," she laughed. "And I didn't see you refusing the port he didn't want to go bad in the bottle!"

Munro grinned, awake now, and entertained. "It's good that he's making healthier choices; I'm only supporting him. Anyway, why are you so worried about what I was drinking?" he asked. "Is my waistline expanding?"

Lana giggled, and pinched his side, secretly pleased to see that he was as lean as ever. She wasn't going to let Munro know that, though.

"There's nothing of you, despite all the cheese, desserts, snacks and second helpings over these holidays. I don't know how you do it; I'll definitely need a decent run today," she opined. "I need to get back into more of a routine. And today we're clearing out the unhealthy things from the fridge," she announced.

Munro sat up, looking alarmed now. "Well, I'm off downstairs to see what we can use up for breakfast," he countered. "Stuart and I like our lazy days with leftovers and treats, you know. He'll be upset if we bin them."

"Oh, Stuart will, will he?" she laughed. "Not you, really? Anyway, I was speaking to Stuart last night about it, and he wants to start coming out with me for a run, so maybe you're not quite so right about that," she teased.

"Subverting my son already?" he gasped. "Treachery!"

They were still giggling and teasing each other as they descended the last few stairs, pleased to see Stuart playing happily with some Lego in his room. As they pottered, preparing breakfast and clearing out the fridge, Lana realised that they were already in a comfortable morning routine, even though it would have to be brought forward when they returned to work and school. They had decided to keep Lana's flat, renting it out through an agency, and she had already moved all her belongings - either into her new home, or into Munro's garage for refurbishment and sale through her business. She was yet to return and finish the deep clean she had started before the wedding - yet to say a final farewell to the flat she loved - but this was now undeniably her home. She smiled to herself, realising that she was happy here and wouldn't miss her own space as much she had once worried. As she started to chop mushrooms and whisk eggs for omelettes, Munro switched on the news.

"Oh!" she exclaimed. "Have they found out who was behind the power cuts yet? Was it environmentalists? I didn't pay much attention yesterday, with the mobile signal down, I just ignored my phone..."

She tailed off as she started to pick up on what was being reported. Munro turned the volume up as the newsreader clarified the situation.

"It has been confirmed by the Home Secretary that yesterday's breakdown of mobile phone services was a concerted denial-of-service attack, linked to the power outages in major cities on New Year's Eve. She stated that it is unknown at this time who might be behind the disruption of these services, or what their motives might be. However, we believe that the attacks are linked to a series of wide-spread emails sent to many UK-based email addresses overnight. Email users have received links to activist websites and video streaming sites. The videos allege an ongoing degradation of human rights in the UK, led by the government. We have received no response to any of our queries about this potential link."

Lana was frowning in confusion and about to check her phone's email when she realised that Munro was ahead of her, laptop open.

"Did you get anything? Do you think it's safe to open?" she asked, softly.

That stopped Munro in his tracks. "That's a good point. Hang on," he muttered, typing quickly, then heading back out of the room. He returned with an ancient tablet and its charger, plugging it into a spare socket on the kitchen counter.

"I have an old email address I haven't used for ages, and no one needs this old thing," he explained. "It's still a bit iffy, as we'll need to be online to view whatever it is, but it's maybe a little bit less risky," he shrugged.

The tablet seemed to take forever to start up, and Lana was surprised at how accustomed she now was to almost-instantaneous access to functionality. She tried to curb her impatience.

"Here we go."

Munro wrapped his arm around her shoulders as she moved to stand beside him, looking down at the small screen propped against the butcher's block which had been too large for her small kitchen, but fitted here perfectly.

"I'm worried..." she started.

"I know," he interrupted, gently kissing her head. "We'll see."

The first link took them to a mostly blank web page, in the centre of which was a video. It auto played after a second; Munro adjusted the volume. The screen showed footage from recent protests, including the ones Lana had attended. The voiceover commenced.

"Not all protests end peacefully, but that's often not the protesters' fault. Not all protests can end peacefully, if the tactics used against legitimate demonstrators are heavy-handed. The UK government is preparing a bill which would make all demonstrations illegal, denying honest citizens the right to protest. Yes, this would stop some few incidents of violence, but it would also take away an important democratic right – the right to voice dissent with how we as a nation are being treated."

The footage had now changed, showing stock images of patients being treated in medical settings. Lana looked to Munro, who widened his eyes in acknowledgment.

"The government are also planning to enforce psychological factorisation testing on us all, starting with those in public-facing roles such as teachers, the NHS, the police and the armed forces. The results of those tests would be used to segregate our society – into those they consider trustworthy, versus those this testing finds lacking. Let us be clear, this is treatment which was designed to help anyone with a mental condition. But now they will use it to judge you, discriminate against you, deny you basic rights and opportunities, and – in some cases – they will use it to remove your freedoms. This is not some baseless scaremongering. In the same email which brought you to this video, you will find links to leaked government documents clearly detailing their plans. If some psychologist says you might one day have a psychotic break, they could lock you up."

Lana's chest was tight, her palms clammy, her thoughts whirling. Munro held her tight, but neither could look away from the footage, as it switched to images of leading politicians.

"How much do you trust these people? You vote them into government, yes. They're a bit of entertainment for many of us. But do you trust them with your life? Do you trust them with your health, your freedom, and that of your families? Do you think these people will be tested and treated the same way as we all shall?" the voice posited.

"On New Year's Eve, we interrupted your parties. On New Year's Day, we stopped you talking to your friends. For that, we apologise. But we needed you to pay attention. We need you to look at the documents we have uncovered for you. We need you to understand the real danger we are all in. Because if we don't rise up, together, now - and stop our government in their tracks - we will lose much, much more than a night out or the ability to call someone. We will lose our right to choose, our freedom to live our lives, and possibly even our freedom itself. We must make it clear that we will NOT be forced into testing. We will NOT be judged and found wanting by some inconclusive means. We will NOT be categorised and classified and denied our rights based on computer programmes and imperfect testers. We will not allow our government to take away our lives as we know them!"

The footage ended abruptly, showing stark images of medical wards, medicated patients staring blankly from wheelchairs and bars on windows. At the foot of the page, links to further pages appeared. Lana gasped, pained from holding her breath while they watched the short message.

"Dear God," she managed to mutter. "Do you think it's all true? Is that the way they're going? How could they?"

Munro shook his head, dismay and disbelief stealing his usual certainty. He clicked his way through the links, reading through each page in detail as Lana peered over his shoulder.

"I'm no expert," he admitted. "But these certainly look legitimate. Bloody hell: this is madness. Surely, there will be a real outcry now."

"Munro," Lana ventured. "Do you think this is still them? Chris and Martha and their people? Do you think...?" She found herself unable to finish the sentence, but Munro knew who she was thinking of.

"I don't know. It could be. She has the passion, and the organisational skills, and maybe even the contacts. This could be what she's been up to, and it would explain why she hasn't been in touch; she wouldn't want us involved in this. I wish she'd talked to us," he added, his deep voice full of regret.

"I think we all know we would have tried to talk her out of this," Lana argued. "And we would all have worried ourselves sick about what she was getting into. I think maybe she knew best, assuming she was sure this was what she wanted to do. Oh!" she suddenly realised. "We'd better let Pete know – he might be completely unaware of this."

Munro nodded his agreement, reaching for his phone, but pausing to turn back towards his wife. "Lana... This is really worrying. For the first time since we got you home, this has me scared for the future. It's so easy to assume that it won't happen. That if it does happen, it won't affect us. That if it does happen, sense will mostly prevail. But who's to say any of that is true? That Stuart will grow up into a balanced, sensible world? Bloody hell," he repeated.

Lana abruptly found their roles reversed. Since the moment they had met, Munro had always been there for her, had always been the solid rock to which she could hold during the worst of her times. Now, she could see his fear for his family, see his uncertainty and need for comfort. She took his hands, knowing it was her turn to reassure him. She looked up into his eyes, somehow finding the courage for them both. They would be fine, together, with their families and friends beside them. That was how they were meant to be, and surely everything else would be okay because of it.

Epilogue

The hot, dry breeze rattled through the desiccated grasses, hissing through the stalks and lifting clusters of fluffy seeds high into the air from their drooping perches above their leaves. It had been a typical English summer's day, the sky scorched bronze by the sun, the air baking and still. But now, with the day just ended, fresher air was coming in from off the channel, bringing salt tang and cooling comfort along with the body odour of the others to her right. Lou lifted her head a little, keeping it mostly below the level of the rocky outcrop which hid her, but straining for fresher air, nevertheless.

In the distance, she could hear a few sheep bleating their woes, perhaps some lucky citizen granted the right to keep the rare creatures. She had heard rumour of a historical enclave nearby, one of those closed villages set up to mock the olden days which no one alive remembered, but so many still craved. The posh and the privileged would come to visit in the cooler season, playing at being pastoral. Perhaps it was that; this marsh had held countless sheep for centuries before this, before the rivers were polluted and the tides too salt for even the toughest of ewes to endure.

Bringing her gaze back into focus, she spotted movement to her left, instinctively freezing before she realised the scale of the activity. She lifted her glasses, peering through them, one eye scrunched up to accommodate the skewed focus which could no longer be adjusted. One side of her mouth lifted in surprised delight as she watched the field mouse scarpering across the dried turf which separated two stands of reeds. Its furtive dash reminded her uncomfortably of her own movements that night, and their purpose here.

She checked the watch on Cree's arm, beside her. The leaders had been gone under an hour, but their parlay should end soon. The longer they stayed in any one place, the more likely they would be discovered. She shook herself mentally, nodded at Cree's unspoken question, and focused once more on the night. Each half hour, they changed their observations, swapping ground level for the skies and vice versa, but she didn't think she'd need to do another full shift after this one; they'd be heading out before then. No one liked being assigned sky-watch first: at night, the eyes tired of gazing at the flat, glazed, darkness. Lou privately thought that some ancestral memory was made uncomfortable by the lack of stars, the pollution that screened them rarely dissipating.

A soft crunch of crumbled concrete and brick caught her ear, and she once again pulled up the glasses. The sound had come from the same direction as the parlay, perhaps the old foundations which stood just in front of the stand of trees which shielded the meet. As she peered into the night, shapes shifted, merged and resolved in her sight like phantoms, but she could see nothing real to cause alarm. The noise was unexplained, however, so she stopped scanning the wider area to see if it was repeated. Her mind wandered as she watched, turning over the minutiae of her day. Tern had sat beside her at assembly again, their knees brushing as they listened to the whispered reassurances and convocations of the morning rituals. After, as they separated to attend their training sessions, their fingers had brushed, releasing a frisson of goosebumps up Lou's arms. Now she winced, knowing she was behaving like a kid, irritated at the lack of focus her distracted mind could achieve. She shut her eyes for a few seconds to refresh her night vision, then looked up and across the horizon. She couldn't control the intake of horrified breath she took.

"Factors!" she cried. "Helmet and goggles, South-East of four, two hundred metres!"

Everyone knew the protocol; everyone knew the locations of the numbered teams and the compass points that would be most relevant to each. They would scatter, every person for themselves, knowing only what had been spotted and roughly where. Lou and her team, as shouters, stayed low – knowing the risk of being located by her call, but accepting that this would only be worsened if they moved at this stage. They couldn't risk the other teams.

As shots began to be fired, close to where team three had been situated, Lou, Cree and the others of her team started their slow reverse, keeping low to their stomachs until they were in the dry, sandy drainage channels they had followed from the farthest reaches of the old marsh. They ran, bent over at the waist, slowly separating to reduce the risk of being caught in numbers. She saw Cree go to ground, squeezing into what must have been an old animal hole, and didn't envy him the hours, perhaps days, of fearful waiting. She continued to run, as the fighting became more intense, gun shots and shouts of pain and anger echoing across the usually empty landscape.

Factors, she rued. How had they found them? They'd come from any number of secure locations, travelling for days, stopping often to ensure they weren't followed. How had anyone been tracked right to the meet? What if the parlay had been surrounded? What if the leaders - from all five southern sectors - had been caught? She swallowed the panic she felt rising, finding strength in the thought of the training they had all persisted with. Everyone knew the protocols; everyone knew their way out and the precautions to take.

She ran, stopped, ran, thankful that she hadn't yet been found or had to fight. She kept it up, somehow finding the energy to keep going until she was miles away from the meet site, skirting the inhabited towns and aiming for the first of the hideys she would use over the next few days. She certainly wouldn't be followed back home, she vowed.

Factors! she thought yet again. How could they live with themselves? Hunting and trapping their fellow men, reducing them to a sub-human status just because they chose to live their own life, un-tested and un-treated. People - flesh and blood just like her - but so indoctrinated in the divisive ways of their tilted world that they couldn't see how lucky they were to have homes, food, even families, if they were granted permission. Factors - running around finding anyone who dared to live without their ID trackers, dragging them off to be psych tested and labelled and penned into whatever enforced community they were deemed suitable for. Drugs in the water and food supplies, no choice that wasn't made for them by the privileged norms in government. It was a fate that horrified Lou, and she never once felt anything but entire gratitude that she had been born wild and raised in the care of the resistance.

"Bev's grief," she muttered, as she scanned the valley

she needed to cross. "I need water, and I need to sleep. Please let me get to the hidey safely. Please let me get home. Please don't let me have to kill a man. Please let the others be okay. Bev's grief, protect us," she concluded, tucking her scarf tightly into her jacket, and slinking down past the ruined farm buildings towards the safer woodland across the way. It would take her days, but she would get home, she would tell her tale. One of these days, one of these fights, one day - eventually - they would take back their country and give freedom back to every single person who wanted it. This, she swore every morning, and tomorrow would be no different.

Afterword

Thank you for reading this second instalment in The Factors series; I hope you've enjoyed reading it as much as I enjoyed writing it! If you have a chance, please leave a review on Amazon - I appreciate your feedback so much.

I have more stories to come in this series, but my next novel will be something a little different, as I experiment with different characters and styles. Hopefully you will enjoy the change of scene as much as I do! You can always find the latest news about my work at www.salhunter.com

As always, my writing draws on some of my own past experiences, and reflects some real locations, but everything written in these pages is make-believe, and all my characters are entirely fictional.

Thanks again to Carolyn, for all her support as I plod ahead with my writing, and to all my family and friends who are always here for me.

I am – always - most grateful for Ally and Lyall, our home and all the freedom and comforts we have, but could lose so easily.

Sally.

About the Author

Sal Hunter is the author of The Factors series, the first two instalments of which are available on Amazon in both paperback and Kindle editions.

Sal lives on the East coast of Scotland with her family and a vocal Scottie dog. She is inspired by the people and places around her, loving to share her passion for both through her writing.

Find out more at www.salhunter.com

Printed in Great Britain
by Amazon